Dear Reader,

We're thrilled that some of Harlequin's most famous families are making an encore appearance! With this special Famous Families fifty-book collection, we are proud to offer you the chance to relive the drama, the glamour, the suspense and the romance of four of Harlequin's most beloved families—the Fortunes, the Bravos, the McCabes and the Cavanaughs.

Wedding bells are ringing for the infamous Bravos— even if they don't know it yet! The all-American clan created by *USA TODAY* bestselling author Christine Rimmer is the second family in our special collection. Its members are cowboys and billionaires, lawyers and private investigators. Their exploits take them from the mountains of Wyoming to a small, close-knit town in California to the glitzy Vegas strip. But whether they're rich or down-to-earth, city or small-town bred, you'll fall in love with each of the Bravos as they take their own compelling journey to a happy ending.

And coming in May, you'll meet Dr. Jackson McCabe as we introduce you to our next special family, the McCabes of Texas, by beloved author Cathy Gillen Thacker.

Happy reading,

The Editors

CHRISTINE RIMMER

came to her profession the long way around. Before settling down to write about the magic of romance, she'd been everything from an actress to a salesclerk to a waitress. Now that she's finally found work that suits her perfectly, she insists she never had a problem keeping a job—she was merely gaining "life experience" for her future as a novelist.

Christine is grateful not only for the joy she finds in writing, but for what waits when the day's work is through: a man she loves, who loves her right back, and the privilege of watching their children grow and change day to day. She lives with her family in Oregon. Visit Christine at www.christinerimmer.com.

FAMOUS FAMILIES

the
BRAVOS

USA TODAY bestselling author

CHRISTINE RIMMER

Scrooge and the Single Girl

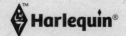

TORONTO NEW YORK LONDON
AMSTERDAM PARIS SYDNEY HAMBURG
STOCKHOLM ATHENS TOKYO MILAN MADRID
PRAGUE WARSAW BUDAPEST AUCKLAND

In loving memory of
the house my mother was born in, a house
we filled with our family memories,
the house we always called the
Old House.

Recycling programs
for this product may
not exist in your area.

ISBN-13: 978-0-373-36503-6

SCROOGE AND THE SINGLE GIRL

www.Harlequin.com

Printed in U.S.A.

FAMOUS FAMILIES

The Fortunes

Cowboy at Midnight by Ann Major
A Baby Changes Everything by Marie Ferrarella
In the Arms of the Law by Peggy Moreland
Lone Star Rancher by Laurie Paige
The Good Doctor by Karen Rose Smith
The Debutante by Elizabeth Bevarly
Keeping Her Safe by Myrna Mackenzie
The Law of Attraction by Kristi Gold
Once a Rebel by Sheri WhiteFeather
Military Man by Marie Ferrarella
Fortune's Legacy by Maureen Child
The Reckoning by Christie Ridgway

The Bravos by Christine Rimmer

The Nine-Month Marriage
Marriage by Necessity
Practically Married
Married by Accident
The Millionaire She Married
The M.D. She Had to Marry
The Marriage Agreement
The Bravo Billionaire
The Marriage Conspiracy
His Executive Sweetheart
Mercury Rising
Scrooge and the Single Girl

The McCabes by Cathy Gillen Thacker

Dr. Cowboy
Wildcat Cowboy
A Cowboy's Woman
A Cowboy Kind of Daddy
A Night Worth Remembering
The Seven-Year Proposal
The Dad Next Door
The Last Virgin in Texas
Texas Vows: A McCabe Family Saga
The Ultimate Texas Bachelor
Santa's Texas Lullaby
A Texas Wedding Vow
Blame It on Texas
A Laramie, Texas Christmas
From Texas, With Love

The Cavanaughs by Marie Ferrarella

Racing Against Time
Crime and Passion
Internal Affair
Dangerous Games
The Strong Silent Type
Cavanaugh's Woman
In Broad Daylight
Alone in the Dark
Dangerous Disguise
The Woman Who Wasn't There
Cavanaugh Watch
Cavanaugh Heat

Chapter 1

Jillian Diamond left Sacramento at a little after two on that cold, clear Sunday afternoon in late December. She was barely out of town before the sky began to darken.

In the foothills, a light snow was falling. The fluffy flakes blew down, swirling in the gray sky, melting the instant they hit the windshield.

Jilly cast a quick glance at the seat beside her. "Voilà, Missy. Snow."

Miss Demeanor, a small calico cat with one mangled ear and an ordinarily pleasant disposition, glared at her mistress through the screened door of the carrier that held her prisoner. Missy did not enjoy traveling.

Jilly faced the road again and continued, as if Missy cared, "Snow is good, you know that. Snow is part of the plan."

The plan was this: Take one creative, contented single

woman, add Christmas in an idyllic setting, mix well and come up with…a column. Or maybe an article, something suitable for the slicks. Options, at this point, were wide open.

And no, this was not to be your usual desperate, club-hopping *singleton's* Christmas, not your ho-hum lonely career girl wandering aimlessly in a coupled-up world, with humor. Not your predictable tale of meaningless sexual encounters with guys who have it all—except for a heart. That was only what Jilly's editor at the *Sacramento Press-Telegram* had asked for in the first place.

Jilly had told him no way. "Listen, Frank. I don't care if half the time it seems to me that that's my life, exactly. It's not going in the *Press-Telegram* for everyone I know—not to mention two hundred and fifty thousand strangers—to read about." She'd shot back a counterproposal: the *happy* single girl's Christmas. That is, Jillian and her cat and a Christmas tree, perfectly content all on their own, in some quiet, scenic, isolated place.

Frank had had the bad taste to stifle a yawn. "On second thought, never mind."

So fine. Jilly decided she would do it on spec and sell it next year.

Which was why she and Missy were all packed up in her 4Runner, heading toward a certain secluded old house high in the Sierras, on the Nevada side of Lake Tahoe.

And the weather was cooperating nicely. Because, of course, for Christmas with the contented single girl, there should be snow, and it should be drifting attractively down outside a big picture window.

Too bad Jilly got going on this project a little late, thus necessitating settling for a setting a tad less than ideal. Most likely, there wouldn't be any picture windows in this particular house. But Jilly was okay with that. She'd have mountains and pine trees and lovely, sparkly white snow. For the rest, she'd make do. She fed a Christmas CD into the stereo, pumped up the volume good and high and sang right along with Boyz II Men.

"Let it snow, let it snow, let it snow...."

Which it did. The snow came down harder. Thicker. It was starting to stick, too. Jilly turned on the wipers and slid in another Christmas CD.

By the time she reached Echo Summit, she found herself driving through a true snowstorm. But the Chains Required signs weren't up yet. Traffic was still moving right along. And she had four-wheel drive, so she was doing all right. Night was falling. Her headlights, set on auto, switched themselves on.

It was after she left the highway, not too far beyond Tahoe Village, that things started to get scary. But not *too* scary. She was handling it. At first.

Caitlin Bravo, a stunning and frequently overbearing woman on the far side of fifty, owned the house Jilly was looking for. Caitlin had provided detailed instructions for finding the place. There were a number of small, twisting mountain roads to navigate, but Jilly had it all mapped out. It should have been a piece of cake.

It *would* have been a piece of cake. In daylight, minus the blizzard.

Jilly turned off the Christmas music and tried the radio, but almost ran herself off the road in her effort to tune in the weather and drive at the same time. And really, she'd gone a little past the point where a weather report would do her much good. The view out her windshield told her more than she wanted to know. She should have checked the forecast a little earlier—like before she left Sacramento. It was a problem she had and she knew it. Sometimes she'd forget to look into important details in her enthusiasm to get going on a project that enticed her.

"So shoot me," she muttered as she switched off the radio. She focused all her concentration on the snake-like, narrow road as it materialized before her in the glare of her low beams. She was deep in the forest now, pines and firs looming thick and shadowed on either side of the road.

She missed a turn and didn't realize it until five or six miles later. Slowing to a crawl so she wouldn't miss it again, she backtracked, searching. She found it. And then missed the next one, had to backtrack, found the turn at last, felt her flagging spirits lifting—only to realize she'd missed *another* one.

On the seat beside her, Missy was not pleased. Irritated whines had begun to issue from the cat carrier.

"Missy honey, I am doing the best I can, all right?"

The cat only meowed back at her, a petulant sort of sound.

"I'll get us there, I promise you. And then it's a nice, big bowl of Fancy Feast for my favorite girl."

Missy said nothing. Just as well. Jilly needed all her attention focused on the next turn—which, for once, she actually found the first time around. She drove on, winding her way up and down the sides of mountains.

At last, at a few minutes after six, a good hour past the time she should have reached it, she found the rutted, snow-drifted dirt driveway that led to her destination. Her stomach growled. She thought of the bags of groceries in back. They contained ingredients for a number of gourmet meals. Gourmet, after all, had seemed the best way to go for this project.

Too bad what she longed for right now was some Dinty Moore chili, or maybe a big can of—

Jilly let out a startled cry and stomped on the brake as a doe leapt from the cover of the trees and directly into her path.

Luckily, she managed to stop before she hit it. And then it did what a deer always does. It froze directly in front of her vehicle and stared into the beams of her headlights, an expression of total surprise and dumb-animal disbelief in those big, sweet, bulging brown eyes.

Jilly rolled down her window, stuck her head out into the freezing storm and yelled, "Go on, you! Get out of here! Get lost before I make a jacket out of you!"

The doe blinked and took off, disappearing into the leafless bushes and pine trees at the other side of the driveway. Jilly pulled her head back inside, rolled up the window and brushed the snow out of her hair. Then she drove on, straining to see, the snow hitting the windshield so hard and thick, there was nothing but whiteness three feet beyond her front bumper.

The driveway was very long. Or at least, it seemed that way in the dark, with near-zero visibility. Jilly rolled along with great care, hunched over the steering wheel, peering into the wall of white in front of her, trying not to run into a pine tree or another startled deer.

Okay, truth. She was getting worried. She could end up snowed in up here in the middle of nowhere, with nobody but Missy to turn to. "Oh, not good," she murmured under her breath. "Not good at all...."

But then she reminded herself that she did have her cell phone, that people knew where the old house was and knew she was headed there. She would be all right. She could call for help and get it eventually if it turned out she really needed it.

However, on the subject of the house, where *was* it? What if she'd somehow managed to miss it? What would happen if she—

And right then she saw it.

"Oh, thank you," she cried. "Thank you, thank you, thank you, God!"

Not twenty feet ahead, the driveway opened out into a clearing. And in the middle of the clearing she could make out the looming shadow of the old house, with its high-pitched roof and long, deep porches. Smoke trailed up from the chimney-pipe and the golden light inside shone like a beacon through the swirling, blinding—

Wait a minute.

The golden light inside?

The house was supposed to be unoccupied.

Jilly reached the clearing. She pulled in beside the vehicle already parked there. Then she turned off the engine and sat for a moment, staring at the lighted house as snow gathered on the windshield, obscuring her view. Who could be in there? What in the world was going on?

About then she turned her head and looked through her side window at the other car. The window was fogging up. She rubbed at it with her open palm and peered closer.

"Omigod."

It was Will Bravo's car. She was sure of it. It was a very distinctive car, the Mercedes Benz version of a sport utility vehicle. Silver in color. What did they call it? A G-Class, she thought.

Will Bravo's car.

Jilly shivered. Will was Caitlin's middle son. The *only* one of Caitlin's three sons who remained a bachelor, the other two having married Jilly's two dearest friends, Jane Elliott and Celia Tuttle.

Will Bravo's car....

Everything was starting to make way too much sense. "Caitlin, how could you?" Jilly whispered under her breath. She felt tricked. Used. Thoroughly manipulated.

She grabbed her purse from the floor in front of the passenger seat and fumbled through it until she came up with her phone. She'd stored Caitlin's number, just in case she might need it. She punched it up. But when she put the phone to her ear, instead of ringing at the other end, all she got was static.

Jilly yanked the device away from her ear and glared at it. Terrific. So much for being able to count on her cell.

Missy meowed.

Jilly shoved the phone back in her purse, stuck her

arm over the seat and got her coat and hat. She pulled on the coat and jammed the hat on her head. Then she hooked her purse over one shoulder, grabbed the cat carrier, leaned on her door and climbed out into the raging storm.

Chapter 2

Will Bravo was just about to sit down to his solitary dinner of franks and beans, with a copy of *Crime and Punishment* for company, when someone knocked on the kitchen door.

What the…?

His grandmother's cabin was off the beaten path in every way. To get there, you had to have directions. Even when the weather was good, nobody ever just dropped in. Which was why he was here in the first place. He wanted to be left alone.

Whoever it was knocked some more.

Will went over and pulled open the door, and Jillian Diamond blew in on a huge gust of snow-laden wind. She was wearing a red wool hat, a big shearling coat, faded overalls, lace-up boots and a red-and-green striped sweater with a row of red reindeer embroidered on the turtleneck collar. In her left hand, she clutched an animal carrier from which suspicious meowing sounds were issuing.

Will couldn't believe this. "What the hell are *you* doing here?"

Now, wasn't that going to be fun to explain? Jilly thought. She caught the door and pushed it shut, then set Missy's carrier on the warped linoleum floor, sliding her purse off her shoulder and dropping it next to her unhappy cat.

"I asked you what you're doing here," Will demanded for the second time.

She didn't know where to start, so she countered provokingly, "I could ask you the same question."

He studied her for a moment, his head tipped sideways. And then he folded his big arms across his broad chest and informed her, "I'm here every year from the twenty-second or twenty-third until the day after New Year's."

Jilly swiped her hat off her head and beat it against her leg to shake off the snow. "Well, sorry. I honestly didn't know."

He grunted. "You could have asked anyone. My mother—" Oh my, Jilly thought, surprise, surprise. "—my brothers. Even, more than likely, your two best friends."

"Oh, really?"

"Yeah. Really."

"Well, this may come as a rude shock to you, but asking if you were going to be here never even occurred to me." Yeah, okay. Maybe it *should* have occurred to her. Given what she knew about Caitlin Bravo, it all seemed achingly obvious now. But that was called hindsight and it and 3.49 would get you a *venti* latte at Starbuck's.

He was glaring at her, as if he suspected her of all kinds of awful things, as if he didn't believe a word she had said. She didn't even want to look at him.

So she didn't. She looked away, and found herself staring at the single place-setting and the thick hardbound book waiting on the ancient drop-leaf table about three feet from the door. Delicious comfort food smells issued from the pot on the stove.

"Answer my question," he growled at her. "What are you doing here?"

From the carrier, Missy meowed plaintively. "Look," Jilly said with a sigh. "I'm sorry to have disturbed you. I swear I didn't have a clue that you were going to be here."

He made a low scoffing sound. Jilly could see it all, right there in his gorgeous, lagoon-blue eyes. He thought she was *after* him. He believed she *had* known that he was staying here, that she'd followed him up here to the middle of nowhere to try and hook up with him.

She threw up both hands. "Think what you want to think. The deal is, though I truly hate to put you out, it's very bad out there. I'm stuck here for the night and we both know it."

He did more scowling and glaring. Then at last he gave in and muttered grudgingly, "You're right. You're going nowhere tonight."

Oh, thank you so much for admitting the obvious,

she thought. She said, "Right now, I need to get a few things in from my car." Missy meowed again. "Like a litter box and some cat food, for starters."

"All right. That's reasonable." Various coats and wool scarves hung on a line of wooden pegs beside the door. He grabbed a hooded down jacket. "Let's go."

Nothing would have given her more pleasure than to tell him she didn't need his help. But there was her pride—and then there were her suitcases, the cat supplies and the various exotic lettuces and veggies and the hormone-free fresh turkey she'd brought to roast for her happy single-girl's Christmas feast. And what about that bottle of good pinot grigio she'd bought to enjoy with her Christmas dinner, not to mention the pricey champagne she'd bought to toast the New Year? No way she was leaving them outside to freeze. If she trekked everything in alone, it would take two trips, maybe three. And it really was cold out there.

"Thank you," she said tightly as she stuck her hat back on her head.

Outside, even under the protection provided by the porch, the icy wind seemed to cut the frozen night like the blade of a bitterly sharp knife. Once they moved off the porch and into the open clearing, it got worse. They struggled against the wind, getting beaten in the face with freezing snow, finding no shelter as they passed beneath the single bare maple tree between the vehicles and the house. It wasn't really all that far; it only felt like a hundred miles.

When they reached the cars at last, she went around to the rear of her Toyota and lifted the hatch. She passed him a twenty-pound bag of cat litter and another bag containing cat food and a plastic litter box. He managed to handle all that with one arm, so she also gave him the smaller of her two suitcases—it had her pjs in it, and a change of underwear, all she'd need for one night. Then, after giving him a backhanded wave meant to dismiss him, she turned to the bags of groceries and started going through them, consolidating the food items that had to go inside.

Will hadn't budged. "What the hell are you doing?" he yelled at her over the howling of the wind.

"Just go on inside!" she shouted back.

But of course, he didn't. What was it about some men? Congenitally incapable of following instructions.

"I asked you what the hell you're doing!"

So she told him. "Perishables!"

He didn't say anything after that. Just stood there, looking at her, eyes narrowed, mouth turned down at the corners, ice collecting in his bronze eyebrows, his ears and that handsome blade of a nose turning Rudolph-red.

Jilly turned back to her bags of groceries. It didn't take all that long to get everything that wouldn't hold up in a freezing car down to four plastic bags—one of them being the turkey. She hefted the bags out of the car and shut the hatch.

"Here," Will shouted. "Give me—"

"No," she hollered back. "I've got the rest. Let's go."

He gave her another of those dark, mean looks he was so good at. Now what? He was peeved because she wouldn't let him carry the heaviest load? Was there no end to reasons for this man to be mad at her?

She turned her back on him and started for the porch. He was right behind her when she got to the front door. She set down the bags in her right hand to reach for the knob—and his hand came around and grabbed it first. She resisted the urge to glare at him over her shoulder. He pushed the door inward. She picked up her bags again and stepped inside.

It only took a few minutes to set up Missy's comfort station in a corner of the bathroom, which was right off the kitchen. She let the cat out of the carrier as she dished up the Fancy Feast and filled a water bowl.

Once Missy was taken care of, Jilly joined her in the bathroom, shutting the door on Will, who was standing by the ancient drop-leaf kitchen table, staring bleakly at the bags of groceries.

Jilly used the facilities and washed her hands. When she entered the kitchen again, he'd moved her grocery bags to the long counter beside the darling, classic-looking round-sided Frigidaire. "What is this turkey doing in here?" he demanded.

"The rumba?" she suggested cheerfully.

He opened the Frigidaire and began stashing her lettuce and vegetables inside. "You know what I mean. You could have left it in your car."

"No way. If I'd wanted a frozen turkey, I would have bought one. That's a free-range, all-natural *fresh* turkey and it's going to stay that way."

He grumbled something under his breath. She couldn't make it out and decided it was probably better if she didn't try. He moved stuff around on one of the shelves in the fridge, then he picked up the turkey, stuck it inside and shut the door. "All right. Your cat is taken care of and the food's put away. I'm going to eat now. It's only franks and beans, but you're welcome to join me."

Oh, how she longed to hold her head high and refuse. But Jilly really loved franks and beans. As far as she was concerned, franks and beans ranked right up there with Dinty Moore chili. With Kraft mac and cheese. With bacon burgers. With her hands-down favorite of all time: Cheez Doodles.

And speaking of Cheez Doodles, she had several bags of them stowed out in the 4Runner. She should have thought to bring some along when they were lugging everything else inside.

"Do you want the food or not?" her ungracious host inquired darkly.

"Yes," she said. "I do."

He got down a plate, dug a fork out of a drawer. "Milk?"

"Yes, please." She found a glass in a cupboard and poured it for herself. Then they sat down, put their paper napkins in their laps and dug in.

Oh, it was heaven. She hadn't realized how hungry she was. With effort, she restrained herself from making ecstatic groaning noises. At that moment, eating the hot, lovely food, she could almost be grateful that she'd found Will Bravo here, that she hadn't arrived to find it all dark and deserted, had to start the fire herself and worry about being all alone out here in this creaky old house while a blizzard raged outside and her cell phone was on the blink.

But then she looked up and caught him glaring at her and all her good will evaporated.

He said, "Now tell me. Why are you here?"

She shoved in another mouthful of beans, chewed them and swallowed. Then she gulped a little milk. Let him wait, she was thinking. It's not going to kill him. Outside, the wind wailed.

Will went on scowling. Good gravy. How could she ever have imagined she might get something going with him?

And okay, she'd admit it. At one time—up until just a couple of weeks ago, as a matter of fact—she'd cherished the doomed hope that she and Will might get it together.

They had seemed to have a lot in common. Both from the same hometown, which was New Venice, Nevada, in the Comstock Valley, about twenty miles away from this dreary old house, down a number of twisting, turning mountain roads. They had both settled, at least for now, in Sacramento. And then there was the most obvious connection: his two brothers had married her two best friends.

And also, well, she might as well admit it. She'd been blinded for a while there by the kinds of minor details that have made women fools for certain men since the dawn of time. Blinded by things like his good looks and his social veneer—okay, it was hard to believe, looking at him now, but Will Bravo could be a major charmer when he chose to be. And along with the charm, he had that slightly dangerous rep as one of those yummy bad Bravo boys. Oh, and she mustn't forget his impressive professional credentials: Will was an up-and-coming attorney on the Sacramento scene. For a while there, she'd dared to imagine that just maybe Will Bravo could turn out to be the man of her dreams.

But not anymore. Her eyes were wide open now. She saw him for what he really was: sour, sad and angry. Lost and alone—and determined to stay that way.

So let him. Tomorrow, when the storm was over, she'd pack up her Toyota, put Missy in her carrier and make tracks for home.

"Jillian," he said in a low, warning tone.

She set down her glass and wiped her mouth with her napkin. "All right. It was like this. I needed an isolated cabin for a holiday piece I'm working on."

He was staring at her, a sneering curl to his mouth. She knew what he thought of her. That she was shallow, one-dimensional, flighty in the extreme.

Far be it from her to disappoint him. "Originally, of course, I imagined a place with cable and central heat and a nice view of Lake Tahoe. One with a fully equipped kitchen and chef-quality appliances." She waved her fork airily. "Unfortunately, it's just been too crazy lately. One project after another, if you know what I mean. By the time I got around to making the arrangements, options were limited. More than limited. I couldn't find a place."

"So you called my mother."

"No. First, I called Celia."

He blinked. Then he gave out grudgingly, "Makes sense."

And it did. Celia Tuttle, who was now Celia Bravo,

had spent most of her working life as a personal assistant, first to a television talk-show host and then to the man who was now her husband, Will's brother, Aaron. It was part of Celia's job to know how to find just about anything anyone might need on very short notice.

"Celia reminded me about this house," Jilly told him.

"And suggested that you give Caitlin a call." He was getting the whole thing into perspective now, she could see it in his face. He was accepting the fact that she had been tricked every bit as much as he had.

Caitlin Bravo was a hopeless matchmaker when it came to her sons. And Aaron and Cade were all taken care of now. Only Will had yet to find a wife.

The son in question nodded wearily. "Okay. You called Caitlin. She offered you this place."

Jilly nodded. "Your mother was smart. She played it just right. She told me all about how primitive the setup would be, reminded me of all the old stories about your grandmother." The house had once belonged to Caitlin's mother, Mavis McCormack, known to everyone in Will and Jilly's hometown as Mad Mavis. People whispered that Mad Mavis's ghost still haunted the old house. "But somehow," Jilly added, "your mother forgot to mention that you would be up here, too. Isn't that surprising?"

"Not in the least." Will stared at the woman across the table from him. She'd taken off her big coat and her funny hat, shoved up the sleeves of her red-and-green turtleneck and dug right into the food he'd offered her. She had wild brown hair with gold streaks in it and sparkly gray-blue eyes under thick, straight, almost-black eyebrows—eyebrows so heavy they should have bordered on ridiculous. Yet somehow, they didn't. Somehow, they looked just right on her.

Attractive? All right, he'd admit it. She was a good-looking woman. If you liked them slightly manic and obsessively upbeat. She had her own business—Image by Jillian, it was called. She counseled fast-track execs and other professional types on how to dress for success—business casual, with flair. She also wrote an advice column, *Ask Jillian*. The column had started out as a weekly, but recently it had gone to Monday through Friday in the *Sacramento Press-Telegram*.

Yeah, he knew all about Jilly Diamond. His mother had made sure of that.

"I'm here every year," he reiterated grimly. "And Caitlin knows it." He was thinking that he wouldn't mind strangling Caitlin as soon as he could get his hands on her. He was thinking that she *deserved* strangling. After all, he'd made it crystal clear to her that Jillian Diamond was *not* the woman for him.

The woman who wasn't for him said, "Well, Caitlin didn't tell me you'd be here, or I promise you, I wouldn't have come."

At first, he'd thought otherwise. The last time he'd seen her, at that party of Jane and Cade's a couple of weeks ago, he could have sworn she was interested. It hadn't been anything obvious. Just the feeling that if he looked twice, she would, too.

He didn't have that feeling anymore. Now, she looked no happier to be stuck with him than he was to have found her at his door.

And that was absolutely fine with him.

He heard a strange, soft rumbling sound and saw something furry in his side vision. Her cat. It had emerged from the bathroom and was sitting beside his chair, looking up at him, eyelids lowered lazily, an expression of near-ecstasy on its spotted face, its orange, black and white tail wrapped around its front paws. The rumbling sound, he realized, was coming from the cat. The damned animal was purring so loudly, he could hear it over the howling of the wind outside.

Jillian said, "Okay, Will. Now *you* tell *me*. What are you doing up here all alone for the holidays?"

He turned from the scary look of adoration in the cat's amber eyes and gave it to her straight. "I hate the holidays. I want nothing to do with them. I accept the fact that there's no way I can avoid this damn jolly season altogether. But I give it my best shot. I decorate nothing. I don't send a single Christmas card. I shop for no one. And I keep my calendar clear from the twenty-second on. I come up here to my eccentric dead grandmother's isolated house. I remain here until January second, without television or an Internet connection, with only a transistor radio to keep up with the weather reports and my mobile phone in case of emergencies." He indicated the Dostoevsky at his elbow. "I catch up on my reading. And I do my level best to tell myself that Christmas doesn't even exist."

She stared at him, one of those too-thick eyebrows lifting. He waited for her to ask the next logical question, which was "Why?" When she did, he would tell her to mind her own damn business.

But she didn't ask. She only said, softly, "Hey. Whatever launches your dinghy."

They did the dishes together, not speaking. She washed and he dried.

As he hooked the dishtowel on the nail above the sink, he said, "There's a bedroom down here, off the living area. I'm in there. You get the upstairs all to yourself." He gestured at the door beside the one that led to the bathroom.

Jilly got her suitcase and her purse and followed him up a narrow flight of steps to a long, dark, spooky attic room. He flicked a wall switch at the top of the stairs. A bare bulb overhead popped on. In the hard, unflattering glare it provided, Jilly took it all in, from the single small window at the head of the stairs to the dingy gray-blue curtain in a pineapple motif at the opposite end.

Someone had taken the time to Sheetrock the slanted ceiling and to paint it and the low walls bubble-gum pink. Too bad they hadn't bothered to cover the nails or tape the seams. The floor was the same as downstairs—buckling speckled linoleum. Three single beds were arranged dormitory style, with their headboards tucked under the lowest line of the eaves.

Oh joy, Jilly thought.

"There's a double bed in the other room." Will gestured at the curtain. "You'd probably be more comfortable in there."

She went through, set down her things and turned on the small lamp by the bed. This area was pretty much identical to the one she'd just left: Sheetrocked and painted pink, with a single dinky window at the end opposite the curtain. The head of the bed butted up under the windowsill.

Will was standing by the curtain. "Everything okay?" He didn't look as if he cared much what her answer might be.

"Fine."

He left her, ducking back through the curtain. She heard his steady tread as he crossed the first room and went down the creaking stairs.

The bed, which was made up already and covered in a threadbare chenille spread, consisted of a set of box springs and a mattress on a plain metal frame. Jilly dropped to the side of it. The springs complained and the mattress sagged beneath her weight. Lovely. She looked at the window and saw her own reflection, ghostly, in the glass. Up here, under the eaves, the eerie sighing of the wind was even louder than downstairs.

She glanced at her watch. It was just seven-thirty. It would be a long, long night.

However. She did have her phone. And she had a few pointed questions for Celia. For instance, did Celia know that Will would be at Mad Mavis's old house? Was Celia in on the matchmaking scheme, along with the devious, domineering Caitlin?

Jilly had a hard time believing that. For one thing, Jilly had never so much as mentioned to either of her closest friends that maybe—just *possibly*—she *might* have considered dating Will Bravo. And she'd also been careful not to ask questions about him. She'd scrupulously avoided showing too much interest when his name came up in conversation.

She did know there was tragedy in Will's past. A few years ago, he'd lost a woman he truly loved. Her name had been Nora. But Jilly had only heard about her in passing.

"Poor Will," Jane had said a month or so ago. "He was so in love. Did you know? Her name was Nora. Cade told me he's still not really over her, even after five years...."

And about a week later, Celia had mentioned that Will and Nora had planned to be married. And that Nora had died before the wedding.

But Jilly never got the details. She didn't let herself ask for them. It had never been anything solid, anyway, those stirrings of attraction she'd felt for Will. And in the end, he'd squashed her feelings flat, leaving her exceedingly glad that she hadn't said a word.

Jilly dug her phone out of her purse and pushed the Talk button—and got the same crackling static she'd gotten earlier, when she'd tried to call Caitlin.

"Wonderful." She tossed the phone down on the bed and let out a groan of frustrated boredom.

She thought of the Cheez Doodles she'd left out in the car. A bag or two could really help to get her through the night. And while she was at it, she could also grab her boom box and CDs. Since Caitlin had warned her that the cabin had no television or stereo, Jilly had brought along the boom box and a thick black zippered folder full of tunes. And not only that. Now that she thought about it, she remembered she'd stuck a few intriguing novels in her overnighter. The evening didn't have to be a total bust, after all.

On the negative side, getting the snacks and the music would mean another freezing excursion out to her car. But not to worry. There *was* good news here. This time she could handle it herself in a single trip. No need to get the scrooge downstairs involved.

Her coat and hat were waiting where she'd left them, on the pegs by the door. She was pulling on the coat when Will said, "What's going on?"

She flipped her hair out from under her collar and reached for her hat. Only then did she bother to face him.

He was sitting in the easy chair in the living area, reading his big, fat Russian novel. He'd dug up an old radio from somewhere and had it tuned in to what sounded like it might be an NPR talk show, though he had it down so low, who could say for sure? Missy lay curled in a ball on the rag rug at his feet, looking as if she belonged there. The cat seemed to like him—a lot. While Jilly understood that cats were contrary by nature, the idea of her own sweet Missy developing a kitty crush on Will Bravo didn't please her at all. To Jilly's mind, it was carrying contrariness altogether too far, not to mention that it bordered on disloyalty, considering the way Jilly felt about the man.

"I'm going out to my car. I forgot a few things."

He frowned. "It's pretty wild out there. Are you sure you can't get along without whatever it is?"

"Oh, yes. Absolutely. We're talking utter necessities." She smiled brightly and gave him an emphatic nod.

He was slanting her a doubtful look. "You need some

help?" He didn't sound terribly anxious to get up from that comfortable chair and trudge out into the freezing, windy darkness.

But at least he had offered. She said, more pleasantly than before, "No, thanks. I can manage."

He shrugged and went back to his big, boring book.

She pulled open the door and went out into the icy night. A huge gust of wind came roaring down the porch just as she stepped over the threshold, so she had to struggle with the door in order to get it shut. Then she wrapped her coat close around her, hunched her shoulders against the cold and headed for her car.

The snow was thicker on the ground than it had been the last trip out. And the storm itself seemed worse, the wind crueler, the snow borne hard on it, not falling at all, but swooping in sideways, stinging when it hit her cheeks. The branches of the pines that rimmed the clearing whipped wildly, making those strange, ghostly crying noises as the wind rushed between them. Jilly forged on to her car, passing beneath that lone maple tree, hearing those creepy crackling sounds, like bones rubbing together, as the branches scraped against each other.

At the Toyota, she hauled up the hatch and crawled inside. She got the boom box from the back seat, then climbed over that set of seats and got the CD folder from where she'd left it on the front passenger side. Then she backed out, grabbing a bag of Cheez Doodles on her way. She almost reached for her laptop, too. But it would just be something else to drag back outside tomorrow morning when she loaded up to leave, so she vetoed that idea.

Easing her boots down to the snowy ground, she got the hatch shut. She had the CD folder tucked under an arm and the boom box and the bag of cheese snacks in either hand as she started for the house.

She got as far as the big maple tree when a particularly hard gust of wind struck. She heard a sharp, explosive sound and glanced up just in time to see the heavy bare branch come crashing down on top of her.

Chapter 3

That cat of Jillian's got up and stretched. It had started purring again. Loudly. It sat and licked its right front paw for a minute or two, then swiped the paw twice over its tattered ear. And then it just sat there, looking up at him. Adoringly.

Will found the situation nothing short of unnerving. "Get lost," he growled.

The cat didn't move. The purring, if anything, seemed to grow louder. Mentally, Will drew the line. If that animal started rubbing itself against his leg, he was going to kick it. Firmly.

He didn't like cats. Or dogs. Pets in general left him cold. Strangely, most animals seemed to like him. He didn't get it. He just wished they would leave him alone.

The cat rose up on all fours and took a step toward him.

"Don't," he said loudly.

The cat dropped to its haunches again and went back to staring and purring with low, dreamy eyes. Will stared back for another two or three seconds, a hard stare, a stare meant to impart how unwelcome he found the attention of animals in general and raggedy-eared calico cats in particular. The cat stayed where it was. He began to feel it would be safe to get back to his book.

He had just lowered his gaze to the open volume in his lap when a particularly hard gust of wind wailed outside. Faintly, he heard that popping crack—like a distant pistol shot. He recognized the sound. A nearby tree had lost a good-sized branch.

He glanced up in time to see the cat blink and perk up its one good ear. Reluctantly, he thought of Jillian. Was it possible that she—?

Ridiculous. No way she could have managed to walk under the wrong tree at exactly the wrong moment. He was just edgy because it was Christmastime, and in his experience, at Christmastime, if something bad could happen, it would.

He shook his head and looked down at his book again. These interruptions were damned irritating. As if he didn't have enough trouble keeping all those Russian names straight even under the most ideal of circumstances.

He read on. One page. Two.

How long had she been out there, anyway? Five minutes? More?

He looked up again. This time he found himself staring at the door, waiting for her to come bursting through it, that mouth of hers going a mile a minute, her arms full of whatever it was she just couldn't last a whole night without.

But it didn't happen. The door stayed closed.

So what? he tried to tell himself. She *was* Jillian, after all. Who knew what went on with a woman like that? She was probably only dithering as usual, fiddling with all those grocery bags, deciding she needed this or that, then changing her mind.

He tried to go back to his book one more time.

But it was no good. She'd been out there too long.

He swore and slammed the book shut.

Jilly blinked. For some strange reason, she was lying down, looking up through the bare branches of a tree at the stormy night sky. The wind was blowing hard and the snow was coming down and it was very cold. Also, she had a doozy of a headache.

She moaned and put a hand to her head, felt something warm and sticky. "Eeuu," she said. "Ugh."

Really, it was too cold to be lying around in the snow.

With effort, she turned over and got up on her hands and knees. From that position, though she found she swayed a little, she could see the tree branch that had hit her. It was directly in front of her. The memory of that split second before impact came back to her. She supposed it was a good thing she'd looked up when she did. As a result, it hadn't landed right on top of her but had only kind of grazed her forehead. She touched the tender, bloody spot again. A goose egg was rising there. Now, that was going to be really attractive.

And wait a minute. Her hair was blowing into her

mouth, plastered against her cheeks. Which meant her hat was gone. Now, where could it have—?

"Whoa," she said as she realized she was listing to the right. She put her hand back down on the freezing snow. It sank in about five inches, all the way to the hard, rocky ground below.

Better, she thought—if, in this situation, there was such a thing. At least on all fours, she could keep her balance.

She turned her head—slowly, since it did ache a lot—to the right. Through the blowing tendrils of her hair, she saw a bag of Cheez Doodles and a tree trunk. She looked the other way, saw her boom box and CD folder and beyond that a ways, an old house.

Ah. She remembered everything now. That was Mad Mavis's house. She was staying there. Just for the night, as it had turned out. Will Bravo was in there, reading *Crime and Punishment,* listening to National Public Radio, and, she hoped, beginning to wonder why she hadn't come back in yet.

But no. Forget Will. He didn't like her. He didn't want her here. It would be a big mistake just to lie here, waiting for him to put down his book and come out and rescue her.

And besides, she was an independent, self-reliant woman and that meant she could take care of herself. She'd got herself into this jam and, by golly, she'd get herself out.

Could she stand?

Carefully, she lifted one hand again—and almost pitched sideways. She put the hand down.

"Ho-kay," she muttered to herself. "Standing up goes in the Doubtful column."

She glanced with regret at her Cheez Doodles. But there was no hope for getting them—or the boom box or the CDs—inside. Not this trip. She needed both hands in order to crawl.

So she started moving, slowly, with difficulty, more dragging herself, really, than crawling. She was thinking that if she could just make it to the porch, she could pound on the wall and Will would come out and help her the rest of the way. He might be a jerk, but he wasn't a total monster. Maybe she could even convince him to go get her Cheez Doodles and her tunes—not that she was counting on that. Oh, no. Just hoping.

She was perhaps a quarter of the way to the porch when she started thinking that maybe she could force herself upright, stagger forward for a while and then go ahead and continue crawling when she fell down again. Yes. That would probably work. She really was feeling less dizzy by the second, which was a very good thing, as the less dizzy she was, the faster she could get herself back inside and out of this bone-chilling cold. She levered up onto her knees.

Miracle of miracles, she stayed there. Her teeth were chattering harder than ever, but she didn't think she was going to fall over just then. She shoved at her unruly, wet hair, pushing it out of her eyes. Next step, bring one foot forward and—

But she didn't get to that, because right then, she noticed that Will was striding toward her through the snow.

In no time at all, he was looming above her. "Damn

it, Jilly." The wind was making a lot of noise, and he spoke softly, for once. But still, she made out what he said.

Hey, she thought. Jilly. For the first time, he'd called her Jilly. Was this progress—or just a wild hallucination brought on by a blow to the head?

She didn't much care. "You know, I have to admit it. I'm really glad to see you."

He didn't reply to that. She wondered if she'd even managed to say it aloud. And then she forgot to wonder as he knelt down and scooped her up into his strong arms, pulling her close to his hard, warm chest. She hooked an arm around his neck and buried her face against his shoulder with a sigh, all the reasons she disliked him for that moment forgotten.

Her head throbbed as he rose to his feet again, but the pain hardly registered. She was just so grateful he had come out and found her. She snuggled closer as he carried her into the house, stopping to stomp the snow off his boots before he went in, kicking the door closed with great authority once they'd crossed the threshold into the warmth and the light.

He took her to the narrow iron bed that served as a sofa and gently laid her down. He tucked pillows tenderly beneath her head. With care, he smoothed her snow-wet hair away from her face, frowning, looking at the goose egg swelling at her temple.

"Is it bad?" she asked.

"I've seen worse." He patted her arm in doctorly fashion. He'd been such a complete crab since she'd knocked on his door that evening, it came as a pleasant surprise to learn that he could drum up a very respectable bed-side manner when he had to.

Her booted feet, still encrusted with snow, hung over the side of the couch. He dropped down there and undid the laces and slid them off. She went ahead and straight-ened herself out on the couch as he stood.

"Right back," he said, and left her. She watched him set her boots by the door and then, still wearing his jacket, he disappeared behind the half-wall that marked off the living area from the kitchen.

She groaned and felt the bump at her temple. Her fin-gers came away smeared with blood. But it wasn't too bad. She strained to look down at herself. Everything in the right place, it seemed to her. And there wasn't that much blood. She could see a few drops on her coat, but nothing to get too worried about.

He returned with an ice pack and a damp cloth, sat down beside her and oh-so-gently began dabbing at her temple.

She winced. "Let me…"

He gave her the cloth. She cleaned herself up. Then he passed her the ice pack. She set the soiled cloth on the table beside her and pressed the ice pack over the bump. It felt good. Soothing.

He peered more closely at her, his brow furrowed. "Do you know who I am?"

That made her smile. "As if I could ever forget."

He actually smiled back—well, almost. There was a definite lift at the corners of his mouth. "Tell me."

"Your name is Will Bravo—and thanks. For coming out and checking on me."

"No problem. Are you hurt anywhere else, except for that bump on your head?"

She considered a moment. "No. Nowhere. Everything's fine."

"Did you lose consciousness?"

"For a minute or two, I think."

He got up again and went through the curtain at the end of the makeshift sofa. He came out with a cell phone, punched a button on it. But when he put it to his ear, he shook his head.

"Not working, huh?"

He turned the phone off and set it down. "I'm afraid you're right."

"I tried mine earlier. It didn't work either."

"The storm, probably—not that cell phones ever work all that well up here."

"How comforting."

"I was going to call 911." His mouth twisted ruefully.

"It's all right. I'll be fine. Though I could use an aspirin or two."

He frowned. "Better not."

She dragged herself to a sitting position. "Because?"

He looked at her for a long moment. "You *are* feeling better."

"I am. Better by the minute." She slipped off her coat, one arm and then the other, switching hands to keep the ice pack over her injury. "If I could just have that aspirin. Or Tylenol. Or—"

"No. You should wait, I think. See if you develop any symptoms." He took the coat from her and went to hang it by the door.

She asked, "Symptoms of...?"

"Serious brain injury."

She pulled the ice pack away from her forehead and gingerly poked at the goose egg. "My brain is fine." He turned toward her again, clearing his throat in such a way that she knew just what he was thinking. "Don't go there," she muttered.

"I don't know what you're talking about—and keep that ice pack on that bump."

"Right. Tell me more about these possible symptoms."

"Things like nausea, disorientation, seizures, vomiting..."

It wasn't going to happen. As she kept trying to tell him, she was just fine. "And if I do develop those symptoms, then what?" He was back to his old self again, glaring at her. She told him what. "Nothing. Because there's nothing we *can* do. We can't call 911. The phones don't work. We can't get out of here because of the storm. We're not going anywhere until tomorrow, at least."

"And your point is?"

"There's nothing to wait for, no medical professionals to consult. What happens, happens—though, as I keep telling you, I'm going to be fine. So could I *please* have a couple of Tylenol?"

He disappeared into the depths of the kitchen. He was back maybe two minutes later, with a glass of water and the pills she'd asked for. She took them. "Thank you."

He waited until she'd set the empty glass on the little

table beside the sofa bed and then he asked, "Where are the things you went outside to get?"

She confessed, "I left them where they fell, under that tree out there. I couldn't carry them and crawl at the same time."

"And what, exactly, are they?"

Reluctantly, she told him.

He grunted. "Absolute necessities, huh?"

"So I exaggerated—and don't worry, I don't expect you to—"

But he was already turning for the door again. She let him go. It wasn't really dangerous out there, between the house and the vehicles—as long as you didn't have the misfortune to be under a tree when it lost a big branch. And what were the odds of that happening again?

No worries. He'd be fine.

And he was. He came back in the door a few minutes later. He had her boom box and her CDs and even her hat. "Your Cheez Doodles must have blown away."

It could have been worse. She thanked him again.

He set her things on the kitchen table and then turned to find her starting to stand. "Stay there."

She made a face at him—but she did sit back down.

He shrugged out of his jacket. "Just lie back and relax for a while."

"I told you, I feel—"

"Jillian. Humor me." He hung the jacket on its peg. "For an hour or so, just stay there on the couch where I can keep an eye on you."

She didn't like the way he said that. As if she were

some spoiled, undependable child who might get into all kinds of trouble if left to her own devices.

Not that she could completely blame him for seeing her that way. After all, she *had* gotten herself into trouble and she was very lucky he'd been around to help out. She had no doubt she would have made it back inside on her own, but it would not have been fun crawling the rest of the way, and her boom box and CDs would still be out in the snow.

So okay. She owed him. She'd do what he told her to do—for an hour. She glanced at her watch—8:05—and then slanted him a look from beneath the shadow of the ice pack. "I'll lie here till five after nine, and that's it."

He said nothing, just went back to his chair, picked up his book, sat down and started reading again.

Jilly plumped up the two skimpy throw pillows and stretched out once more on the creaky old sofa bed. She readjusted the ice pack so it would stay in place by itself, which meant her right eye was covered. She folded her hands over her stomach and stared, one-eyed, at the ceiling.

Like the walls, the ceiling was paneled in wood. What kind of wood, she had no idea. It had all been painted in high-gloss white enamel long, long ago. The enamel was yellowed now and cracked in places.

For a while, as she studied the ceiling, she strained her ears to hear the radio. But he had it turned down so low, all she could make out were two voices speaking with English accents—maybe about world hunger, though there was no way she could be absolutely sure. What in the world, she wanted to ask him, is the point of listening to the radio if you have it down so low, you can't hear what they're saying?

But she didn't ask him. Who cared? She didn't. Let him read his big, fat, pretentious book.

He turned a page. The propane-burning wall heater not far from the kitchen door came on—a click, followed by a rushing sound as the gas was released and set alight by the pilot. Outside, the wind went on howling away.

Jilly sighed. She glanced at her watch—8:17. At this rate, she'd be an old woman by the time the hour was up.

Yes, she knew it. A total inability to lie still and do nothing unless she happened to be asleep was another of her faults. But she would do it. She would keep her agreement with him. Forty-eight more minutes of staring at the ceiling coming right up.

Missy, who'd apparently taken it upon herself to wander into Will's bedroom, came sliding through the split in the curtain—this one printed with palm trees— that served as his bedroom door. She strutted across the black-and-red spotted linoleum, tail held high.

Jilly couldn't resist. She lowered her left hand close to the floor and gestured to Missy to come over and see her.

Will looked up. "Problem?"

"No, not at all." Jilly folded her hands on her stomach again and made herself stare ceiling-ward. But a minute later, she couldn't resist a glance in Missy's direction.

The traitor. She'd found a seat near Will's feet and was looking up at him as if she understood the true meaning of love at last.

Jilly lifted the ice pack briefly in order to check out the bump on her head. It didn't feel all that bad. And her headache really was better. There was no reason at all for her to lie here one minute longer.

Except that she had said she would, *and* that she owed Will and this was what he wanted from her, so that if she went into convulsions or started imagining that she was Napoleon, he would be right there to…what?

To nothing. As she'd kept trying to tell him, if brain damage was in the offing, there wasn't a thing he'd be able to do.

He must have felt her exasperated stare, because he looked up again. "What?"

"Nothing." She carefully set the ice pack back in place, stifled a sigh and took up staring at the ceiling once more.

Decades later, it was 9:05. Jilly set the ice pack on the side table, and swung her feet to the floor.

Will glanced up from his book. "How do you feel?"

"Good. Fine. Incredible."

"Maybe you ought to—"

She put up a hand. "Don't. I did what you wanted. I'm feeling great. May I please be excused?"

He grunted. "All right, Jillian. Go."

I am dismissed, she thought. At last.

She stood. There was a slight throbbing in her temple, but nothing to worry about. Very manageable.

She headed straight for her coat.

She was just reaching to lift it from the peg when he demanded from behind her, "What in hell do you think you're doing?"

Lord, give me strength, she thought. Let me get through this night without murdering this man. She calmly took her coat off the peg.

"Jillian. Are you completely insane? You almost got yourself killed once tonight. You're not giving it another try."

The pure disgust in his voice really got to her. She had a powerful urge to start shouting rude things. But somehow, she managed to keep her cool as she faced him, holding out the coat. "See that? Bloodstains. Once they're set, they're almost impossible to get out. I'm taking this coat in the bathroom and I'm getting to work on these spots."

He blinked. "You're not going outside."

"No. I'm not."

"You're going to spot-clean your coat."

"That's what I said."

"That is the most ridiculous thing I've ever heard."

There was something about the way he said *ridiculous*. She knew what he meant by it. Oh, yes. She did. He meant that *she* was ridiculous.

"Will Bravo. You are pushing me. You are pushing me too far."

"Just put the damn coat back on the peg. Go upstairs and lie down."

"You are so hateful. So bitter. So mean."

"Jillian—"

"It's not my fault a tree branch fell on me. I'm very sorry you had to come out and rescue me."

"I didn't say—"

She waved a hand. "I don't care what you said. *I'm*

saying that I wish you'd just stayed in here by the fire with that damn book of yours. I would have made it in on my own."

"You were barely—"

"I was getting there. All right, it wasn't pretty, but I was managing."

He dared to open his mouth again.

She didn't even let him get a word out. "I want you to listen. I want you to hear me. I am sorry to be here, sorry to disturb you. I was tricked into being here. I swear if I'd had even a suspicion, even a scintilla of a notion that you might be here, I never, ever would have come within a hundred miles of this place."

"I don't care what—"

"I'm not finished. I'm not even close to finished."

He raked a hand back through his hair, and he glared at her good and hard.

As if she cared how hard he glared. He had pushed her too far and he was going to get it.

She hit him with the one thing she would have sworn, until that moment, that she would never, ever have revealed to him. "I heard what you said about me two weeks ago at that party at Jane's."

He actually flinched. Good. He *should* flinch.

"I was right around the corner in the front hall when your mother suggested you ought to go and say hi to that 'sweet little Jillian.' Tell me, Will. Do you happen to remember what you said then?"

"Jillian, I—"

"Oh, no. Please. Wait. Don't tell me. Let me tell you. You said that if you were looking for a woman—which you were not—the last woman in the world you'd go after would be me. Because you find me flighty. That's right. Flighty. Flighty and...how did you put it? Ah. I remember. I'm 'A silly woman with a silly job. A woman of absolutely no depth, a slave to fashion, the kind of woman who would jump over a dying man on the street in order to be at the head of the line when they unlock the doors for Nordstrom's after-Christmas sale.'"

Chapter 4

Jilly noticed with a high degree of satisfaction that Will didn't seem to have anything more to say. There was a long silence, one that crackled with mutual hostility.

Finally, he muttered, "Are you through now?"

"Oh, absolutely. I am done, concluded, finished in the truest sense of the word—and may I please go take care of my coat?"

"Be my guest."

Her head high and her shoulders back, Jilly headed for the bathroom, shutting the door good and hard when she got in there, and then catching sight of herself in the cracked full-length mirror on the back of that door. What she saw was not encouraging. Her hair gave new meaning to the words *matted* and *stringy*. The knot on the right side of her forehead was turning a very unflattering shade of magenta.

Jilly wished a lot of things right then, as she stared at her pitiful reflection in the mirror on the back of the bathroom door. She wished she'd just written the piece Frank had asked for in the first place. Certainly wandering the club scene, guzzling Cosmopolitans, listening to tired pick-up lines couldn't be worse than this. She wished she'd never called Celia about finding a cabin, wished she'd taken a pass on the suggestion that she get a hold of Caitlin—and yes, she *had* been reluctant, after what she'd heard at Jane's party. She wished she'd gone with that reluctance and never picked up the phone.

As a matter of fact, she couldn't wait to get home, to spend Christmas with her own family, after all. Next to what she'd been through up here at Mad Mavis's ramshackle old house, she was actually looking forward to having her mother and her two very married sisters sending her the usual pitying looks, dropping subtle hints about how much happier she'd be if she found someone special, had a baby and did something *worthwhile* with her life for a change.

But wait. What was this?

Looked like a serious case of Poor Me, oh yes it did. And though Jillian Diamond had a number of faults, wallowing around in self-pity was not one of them.

Jilly straightened her shoulders again and carefully smoothed a few straggling strands of hair away from her injury. Okay, it was ugly. But it could have been much worse. And her hair would look a hundred percent better once she'd taken a brush to it.

Too bad her brush was upstairs....

But later for that. First things first. Her coat required attention.

The bathroom lacked the usual white porcelain sink. Instead, two deep concrete laundry sinks lined the outside wall, a long window above them. Jilly turned to the sinks and flipped on the cold water.

As she moistened and blotted the soft suede of her stained coat, she decided that she didn't feel so low, after all. There was something about telling a person the one thing you would have sworn you'd never confess to them that was very freeing. Somehow, it didn't even matter that he hadn't apologized. His response wasn't important.

Jilly bent over her coat, dabbing and blotting. To be fair, she would have to say that he had looked just a little bit embarrassed at what a complete jerk he'd been. She found that appropriate. He *should* be embarrassed.

"There," she said under her breath, holding up the coat and examining her handiwork. "Best I can do until I can get it to the cleaners."

She took the coat back out through the kitchen and hung it at the door, taking scrupulous care not to look in Will's direction. Next, she padded over to the little table by the sofa bed and collected her empty water glass, the bloodstained cloth and the ice pack. She washed the glass, rinsed out the cloth and hung it over one of the bathroom sinks. She emptied the ice pack, leaving it, with the glass, in the dish drainer to dry.

Oh, what she wouldn't give for a long, hot soak in that clawfoot bathtub. But it *was* Will's house—more or less. Somehow, she felt it would be nothing short of rude just to get out her bath salts and fill up the tub without asking him first. And since the last thing she wanted to do was speak to him again, the bath was out. She carried her boom box and CDs upstairs and came back down with her vanity kit. She cleaned her face, brushed her teeth and did what she could with her hideous hair.

Finally, there was Missy to deal with. Jilly carried the litter box and water bowl upstairs. Then she went to get the cat.

As Jilly had feared, Missy was reluctant to leave the newfound object of her inexplicable devotion, but Jilly tempted her with a few cat treats and that was the end of that. She closed the door to the kitchen before she carried the cat up the stairs.

As soon as Jilly put her down, Missy took off. Jilly shrugged and got out her lovely soft micro-fleece pajamas with the blue and yellow stripes on the bottoms and cheerful daisies on the top. She was pulling them on when Missy started crying from the foot of the stairs.

Too bad. She'd get over it.

Jilly slid her Ray Charles *Spirit of Christmas* CD into the boom box, turned the volume low enough that it wouldn't disturb the Grinch downstairs, and got out the three novels she'd brought.

There were two juicy romances and a nail-biting thriller. She chose the thriller. She had no desire at all to read about men and women working out their problems, enjoying great sex and finding lasting love. Not tonight, anyway.

Jilly got under the covers, plumped the pillows against her back and started reading. Eventually, Missy quit meowing pathetically at the stairway door. She appeared at the side of the bed, jumped up next to Jilly, curled in a ball and went to sleep. Outside, the wind wailed and the snow blew against the window, making a sound like someone tapping to get in.

The CD ended. Jilly hardly noticed. The thriller certainly did deliver the goods. It was a tale of a serial killer who murdered young women in various gruesome ways. He broke in on them late at night—they all lived in isolated houses—and no one heard their terrified screams.

The book was probably a bad choice, in hindsight. One of those books that shouldn't be read at night, in the dim attic bedroom of a house rumored to be haunted, with the wind howling outside and a view of a dingy curtain with pineapples on it—pineapples that, somehow, had begun to resemble ghostly faces, grinning malevolently.

"There is nothing to be afraid of," Jilly whispered aloud as she marked her place in the book and set it aside for the night. She was safe in a warm bed. No deranged serial killer lurked outside—and if one did, he certainly should be frozen to death by now. The pineapples in the curtain were not evil faces. Mad Mavis was long gone. And Jilly did not believe in ghosts.

But just to be on the safe side, she left the lamp on. She turned away from the light and snuggled down with Missy purring at her back.

Her headache, she realized, was completely gone. She allowed herself a smug little smile. Take that, Will Bravo. No brain damage for this girl. She yawned.

It wasn't long at all before she drifted off to sleep.

* * *

Jilly woke sometime later. She was lying on her stomach with her face buried in the pillow.

She lifted her head, blinked, and looked out the window above the bed.

The clouds had cleared. The storm was over. A full moon shone in on her, casting a magical, silvery light through the narrow attic room.

And wait a minute. The lamp was off. Odd. Hadn't she left it on?

Jilly pushed herself to her knees and brushed her sleep-tangled hair from her eyes. She picked up her watch from the nightstand and peered at it.

Midnight, on the nose.

Jilly set the watch down and turned over, dragging herself up to a sitting position. She saw Missy, then. The cat was sitting at the end of the bed, golden eyes gleaming eerily in the moonlight, watching her. Jilly stretched out a hand.

And Missy vanished—or rather, she faded away, first becoming transparent and then, poof, gone. Just like that.

Jilly pondered her cat's Cheshire-like disappearance. All was not as it should be.

And who was that skinny old woman standing at the foot of the bed, the one in the quilted blue bathrobe and the ruffled hairnet, the one with the face that vaguely resembled Caitlin Bravo's? The one with Will's blue, blue eyes?

"Mavis?"

The old woman nodded. Imagine that. First, her cat

literally faded away. And now she was being treated to a visitation from Mad Mavis McCormack.

"This is a dream, right?"

Mad Mavis smiled. For such an old, wrinkled woman, she had surprisingly white, straight teeth. She stepped forward—right *through* the bed—and held out her hand.

"Oh, I don't think so," Jilly said.

But Mavis just went on standing there, her lower half disappearing into the bed, holding out that bony hand until Jilly looked down and discovered that she'd taken that hand, after all.

The walls around them were melting, the bed disappearing. Jilly closed her eyes.

When she opened them, she and Mavis still held hands, but now they stood side-by-side. There was another bed in front of them. A man lay sleeping on that bed, facing away from them. Jilly knew who the man was even before she noticed the curtain on the other side of the bed—the one that led to the living area and was printed with palm trees.

"Mavis, I am begging you," Jilly whispered. "Don't do this to me. Okay, maybe for a minute or two, for a fraction of a nanosecond, I *might* have been attracted to him. But not anymore. It's really over, you know? I mean, it never even got started. I don't want anything to do with him. I just want to forget he even exists. And I most certainly don't want him taking up space in my dreams."

Mavis began fading backward, her skinny old hand passing out of Jilly's grip without either of then actually letting go. She floated toward the corner of the room, drifting past the ladder-back rocker under the window, insinuating herself between the far wall and an old dresser with a yellowed lace runner and a streaked mirror in a heavily carved frame.

"Mavis," Jilly hissed. "I am *so* not happy about this."

From the shadows between the dresser and the wall, Mavis gazed at Jilly, mournful reproach in those big, blue eyes.

"Mavis. Let me make myself perfectly clear." Jilly raised her voice to a shout. "Get me out of here!"

But Mavis only stood there—well, hovered there, really. Her pale, bony toes—just visible behind the dark shape of the dresser—didn't quite seem to be touching the floor.

Jilly looked at the dream-Will, lying there on the bed, sound asleep. Her shouting hadn't disturbed him in the least. He turned over with a sigh, but didn't open his eyes.

Okay. She'd admit it. With his eyes closed, not scowling, Will Bravo was a hunk and a half. In this dream of hers, he slept nude—or at least, nude from the waist up. She couldn't tell about the rest of him. The blankets covered that. He had shoulders for days. And beautiful, muscled arms...

"No. Not. No way." Jilly blinked furiously in an effort to make the sleeping, too-tempting Will vanish. He didn't. She insisted, as if anyone was listening, "I said I'm not interested, and I am a woman who says just what she means." She whirled toward the corner where

Mavis should have been hovering. "You had better get me out of—"

But the old woman was gone.

"Jilly." The deep, lazy voice came from behind her.

"Oh, no. Forget it. I am not turning around."

"Jilly…"

"I am not going to look. I am not even going to…" Well, all right, maybe just one little glance.

She sneaked a quick peek. He was sitting up, holding out his fine, long-fingered hand to her, looking at her tenderly, pleadingly. "Jilly."

She gave in and faced him fully. "All right, what?"

He wiggled his fingers at her in a come-hither gesture.

"You can't be serious."

He stared deeply, meaningfully, into her eyes as the sheet, of its own accord, slithered back from his fabulous naked body. Jilly tore her gaze away from those pleading blue eyes and looked lower. Wow. Some dream.

She looked up again, into those tender, pleading eyes and a disembodied voice from somewhere near her left ear said, "Why not?"

"Why not?" she cried. "You've got to be kidding. He doesn't like me. I don't like him."

"Jilly," said the disembodied voice. "Don't you get it? This isn't real. It isn't happening. So what if you hate each other in real life? This isn't real life. This is only a dream."

Jilly considered. While she did that, the dream-Will conveniently froze in place—with his hand out and the covers down to his muscular thighs, looking at her longingly, his manliest attribute pointing proudly ceiling-ward.

"Hmm," said Jilly. It was clear that in this dream he found her overwhelmingly attractive. And she had to admit she really did enjoy having him look at her that way.

Why not just go with it? Why pass up a chance to have him falling all over her for one magical night? Why deny herself? This was one situation where she could do anything she wanted, let this fantasy spin out wherever it wanted to go, and suffer absolutely no consequences after the fact.

There was no "fact." She wasn't here. She was upstairs, sound asleep, dreaming all this.

"Okay," she announced. "I've decided. I'm going with this."

Nobody answered. And Will continued to sit there, still as a statue.

Jilly cleared her throat. "Uh. Hello? Will?"

But he didn't move. He didn't even appear to be breathing. She clapped her hands. Twice.

Nothing.

Terrific. What fun was this going to be?

But wait. This *was* her dream. There had to be some way to—

And it came to her. She put her hand in his.

The room faded and reformed and she found herself on the bed with him, wrapped in those big arms of his.

"I've been waiting for you," he whispered. "For so long." Jilly thought that was carrying the fantasy a little too far, but before she could tell him so, he asked, "You'll help me out, won't you?"

She pulled back a little and peered up at him. "Uh. Help you out, how?"

He didn't answer her question, just gathered her close again, rested his cheek against her hair, and repeated what he'd said before. "Help me, Jilly."

"But—"

"Help me out. God, do I need it."

She pulled back again, intending to explain to him that he really had to get a little more specific or she didn't see how there was much she could do. But before she could say anything, he lowered his mouth to hers.

Good googly-moogly, what a kiss!

He almost burned her lips off. It honestly felt as if steam was coming out of her ears.

When he finally let her come up for air, she realized that her pjs had melted away. She was every bit as naked as he was.

Only a dream, she reminded herself. Only a dream. Enjoy, enjoy…

He guided her back onto the bed, kissing her as they went down. Somehow, it seemed he was kissing her everywhere, every part of her body, all at the same time—her mouth, her neck, lower, and lower still.

Omigoodness. Yes, yes, yes!

His lips were everywhere, all at once. And his hands, well, they were magic hands. He touched every inch of her, found all her most secret, most vulnerable places.

She moaned and she cried out, closing her eyes….

When she looked again, they were joined together.

The bed, the room, everything was gone—everything but the two of them. They moved as one, floating in some warm, soft, enveloping space in the middle of nowhere, all wrapped up in each other, arms and legs entwined. She felt stunned by her own intense pleasure. Everything in that warm place seemed to glow. *They* glowed, Jilly and her fantasy lover, rolling and rippling, rising and falling, forever and ever....

Jilly closed her eyes again.

And they were back in his bedroom, lying contentedly side-by-side. He captured her hand, brought it to his mouth and pressed those wonderful lips of his to the back of it. She actually felt his breath on her skin.

Without stopping to think, she did it again, let her eyes drift shut.

And that time, when she opened them, she found herself lying in the bed upstairs, dressed in her fuzzy pjs once more.

Will had not come with her. Sweet old Mavis was tucking her in, bending close, smiling slightly, blue eyes mysterious and maybe a little bit sad.

Jilly certainly felt sad. "Oh, Mavis. Why do the good dreams always have to end?"

Mavis spoke for the first and only time in Jilly's beautiful, bittersweet almost-Christmas dream. "The dog was named Snatch."

"Huh?"

But nobody answered. Mavis was gone.

Chapter 5

Jilly woke to daylight.

She opened her eyes and stared at the pink ceiling and remembered the strange, lovely dream she'd had the night before. She let out a big sigh. Wouldn't it be something if—

But no. Jilly knew dream from daylight. In the real world, nothing had changed between her and Will Bravo. They disliked each other intensely. They'd been tricked into being here in this house alone together.

And this morning, she would pack her gear and hit the road.

She sat up. And there was Missy, perched in the same spot as last night in Jilly's dream. This morning, however, the cat showed no inclination to begin fading away.

"Rreeow?" Missy rose on all fours and strutted toward Jilly across the chenille spread.

Jilly laughed and caught the cat in her arms. Missy consented to be held. She even purred and reached up a paw to bat Jilly's nose.

Jilly giggled. "Oh, sweetie. Happy Christmas Eve and I love you, too. And you're forgiven your flirtation with Mr. Personality downstairs. Just tell me it's over between you."

Missy was admitting nothing. She continued to purr, looking up at Jilly through those lazy amber eyes.

"Listen here. You might as well start getting over him, because you and I are outta here as soon as I can pack up the car."

Missy had heard enough. She squirmed. Jilly let her go and turned to the window.

It didn't look too promising out there. The storm had passed, yes. But the sky was a threatening gunmetal gray that seemed to warn of more bad weather on the way. Jilly got up on her knees and peered down at the snow on the ground.

It looked…deep. Maybe a foot. Maybe more. From that angle, she couldn't see the vehicles, just the slope of the porch roof, a patch of sparkling-white ground, a lot of pine trees and the snow-covered, evergreen-blanketed mountains all around.

Jilly sank back onto the mattress and bit the inside of her lower lip. Was she snowed in here?

She refused to believe that. Surely the county snowplows would have been at work for hours by now. Maybe the long driveway would still be snowed over, but if she could make it to the road, she should be fine from there.

She had chains—and she knew how to put them on.

In spite of what *some* people thought, she was a capable woman who could do what she had to do to get herself out of a jam.

And being snowed in with Will Bravo definitely qualified as a jam. Jilly shoved back the covers. Time to get up and get going.

"How are you feeling?" he asked when she came downstairs. He was scowling when he said it, which kind of ruined the effect of showing concern for her health.

"I'm fine, thanks."

"There's cereal," he said. "And instant coffee."

He'd set his radio on the kitchen counter, turned up a little higher than last night and tuned—surprise, surprise—to NPR. "Winter came a little late to the Sierras this year," said a voice from the radio. "But no one would argue that it's finally here. Reports are that—"

Jilly tuned it out. The cereal was Froot Loops, and the instant coffee was Belgian crème Cappuccino, and it was as eerie as her dream last night how closely Will Bravo's taste in food paralleled her own.

They sat down at the drop-leaf table. Jilly poured milk on her Froot Loops and stirred her instant cappuccino and told herself she was going to eat quickly, get packed and get out.

Still, as she chewed her cereal and sipped the steaming chocolate-flavored coffee, she just couldn't help shooting sideways glances at her surly host, wondering how any one person could be so utterly awful in real life when just last night, in her dreams, he'd been the sweetest, most tender man in the world—not to mention one heck of a kisser, the kind of lover who never tired, who could kiss every part of her body simultaneously, a man who literally glowed in the dark.

She was about halfway through her cereal when he fisted his spoon and hit the base of the handle twice—hard—on the tabletop, startling her so that she almost choked on a Froot Loop. "What?" he growled, and then, *"What?"* again, as if there was some chance she hadn't heard him the first time.

When she finally managed to swallow and could breathe again, she shouted, "What?" right back at him.

"You keep...looking at me." Those lips that looked just like the wonderful, sensual lips of her dream-lover were curled in disgust—and she *had* to stop thinking about that silly dream.

Right now was what counted. And right now, in the thin light of a cold winter's morn, she could easily toss her instant cappuccino right in his snarling face. "Well, excuse me for breathing. I certainly have no intention of—"

"Just stop it, okay? Just knock it off."

"Fine. Gotcha. No problem at all." She shoved another spoonful of cereal in her mouth and stared with bleak determination into her bowl. She honestly, sincerely intended not to so much as glance in his direction again.

But she couldn't help herself. He astonished her, he truly did. How could anyone be such a complete and total—

She realized she was looking at him again.

He realized it, too. And he was not happy. He muttered something incomprehensible, grabbed his empty cereal bowl and shoved back his chair.

Missy was under there.

She let out a horrible, injured yowl, followed by an angry hiss. Then she took off, so terrified she ran right into the wall.

"You've squashed her tail!" Jilly leapt to her feet. Missy shot off again, this time in the direction of the sofa bed in the living area. "How could you? Poor Missy. She's hurt."

He could not have cared less. He turned for the sink, grumbling roughly, "Keep that animal out of my way."

"Oh, shut up," she cried to his broad back. "Just shut your mean mouth."

Missy had disappeared under the sofa bed. Jilly went after her, getting down on her hands and knees and calling softly, "Missy, come on. Come on, Missy honey…"

But Missy wouldn't come out. She had backed herself way into the far corner among the dust balls and she glared out at Jilly, not budging an inch.

Jilly considered crawling under there and trying to get hold of her, but she didn't want to traumatize her further by grabbing her and dragging her out. Better to get ready, get everything out to the 4Runner, then come back for the cat. She pulled her head out from under the sofa bed and got to her feet again.

In the kitchen, she cleared off her place, washing out her bowl and mug, scrupulously ignoring Will. Once she'd cleaned up after her breakfast, she spent fifteen minutes in the bathroom, brushing her teeth, washing her face, pulling her hair back into a ponytail and applying rudimentary makeup. She indulged in a minute or two of studying the purple knot on her forehead, deciding it didn't look much worse than last night and telling herself to be grateful she didn't have a big shiner to go along with it. It was throbbing just a little.

She found the Tylenol on the shelf above the toilet and shook a couple into her hand. Then she bent over the faucet and gulped enough water to wash them down. That should get rid of her headache—and if it didn't, she knew what would: to get the heck out of here and away from Will Bravo.

When she left the bathroom, she went straight upstairs. She made the bed, packed up her suitcase, grabbed her CDs and her boom box, and marched down the stairs. She'd paused at the door to pull on her boots and get into her coat and hat when Will spoke again.

"What the hell do you think you're doing?"

"Leaving." She crouched to tie her laces.

"Jillian." He let out a very weary breath. She would happily have thrown her boots at him if they weren't already on her feet. "You're not going anywhere."

"Watch me."

"Didn't you hear the radio?"

"I don't care what the radio said."

"Then look outside. It's snowing again. It's going to snow all day. We are snowed in. And we're going to stay that way at least until tomorrow—and very likely until the day after that. The highways are closed. All the roads are impassable. You'll never get ten yards down the driveway."

"I'll manage." She stood and grabbed her coat.

He set his huge book aside and rose from his easy chair. "Jillian. Listen. I'm sorry about your cat."

"Tell that to Missy. She's the one whose tail you crushed."

"Get it through your head, will you?" He spoke quietly—but she could hear the strain in his voice. He was exercising considerable effort not to start shouting again. "We're going to be here, alone together, for a couple of days at the very least. We're going to have to find a way to get along with each other."

She reached for her hat. "A minute ago, you said you were sorry for what you did to Missy. Did you really mean that?"

"I want that animal to stay away from me, but I didn't mean to injure it."

"You're sorry."

"That's what I said."

"Well, I'm sorry, too. But I will go stark, raving out of mind if I don't get out of here and away from you." Jilly jammed her hat on her head, picked up her suitcase, her CDs and her boom box and stomped out the door.

Will winced as she slammed it behind her.

Damn. What the hell was her problem? She would not hear the truth.

So all right. Let her try to leave. It wasn't going to happen. She'd be back inside, driving him nuts with her incessant chatter, her sneaky oblique glances and that irritatingly arousing perfume of hers, within minutes of the time she climbed behind the wheel.

At least it wasn't dark out there. And the wind wasn't

blowing that hard yet. She *should* be able to find her way between the house and her vehicle without having something else fall on her.

And on second thought, why not just sit back and enjoy the five minutes she was away? He sat down in his chair and picked up his book.

His enjoyment didn't last long. About ten seconds later, there she was again, bursting in the door, headed for the kitchen this time. He heard her banging around in the fridge.

She went out again, arms full of grocery bags. He'd read maybe three pages when she returned *again*. That time when she headed back out the door, she was trying to manage both that big bag of cat litter and another bag with God-knew-what in it.

He should have stayed out of it, especially considering that the whole thing was an exercise in purest futility, but somehow he couldn't stop himself from offering, "Look. Do you want some help with that?"

"I can manage, thank you." She set the bag of litter down, opened the door, picked up the bag and went through. The door stayed open for several drafty seconds, no doubt while she juggled the litter and whatever she had in her other hand. Finally, she reached inside and yanked it closed.

Maybe a minute and a half later, it blew open.

Will swore. At length. He started to stand, then dropped back into his chair.

He'd be damned if he was going over there and shutting the damn door for her. She'd be back soon enough. She could shut it herself.

The voice of reason—in general, Will liked to think of himself as a reasonable man—whispered in his ear that he was being every bit as foolish and pigheaded as she was. But there was something about having that woman underfoot round-the-clock that brought his worst qualities to the fore. He started reading again, concentrating fiercely, trying to keep all those Russian names straight, resolutely ignoring the icy wind that was blowing in the door.

And then, out of nowhere, her cat landed on his lap, between his belt and his book.

He reacted on instinct, shouting "No!" raising his book and giving the animal a firm shove off his lap.

Maybe firmer than he should have. The cat went flying. But it landed on its feet. And it ran off into the kitchen, fast, using all four legs, not limping in the least. He was sure he hadn't hurt it—that time, or earlier, when he'd caught its tail under his chair. From what he'd just seen, its tail looked fine.

And where in hell, he wondered, had that woman gotten herself off to?

Outside, he heard engine noises.

What the hell? She shouldn't be trying to drive off yet. Her cat was still in the house with him.

It flew in the face of good sense to pay the slightest attention to what she was up to, but he did it anyway. There was a window about three feet from his chair. He got up and went over there and peeked around the edge of the blind.

The snow was coming down pretty thick by then, but even through the veil of white, he could see the vehicles—and Jillian. She was putting on her chains. Surprisingly, she seemed to have a clear grasp of the process. She'd managed to flatten the snow in the crucial places and she'd laid out the chains. She was just getting ready to drive back onto them. He imagined she might even manage to actually get them hooked correctly in place.

But there was no way even properly installed chains were going to get her down the driveway to the road. The snow was just too damn deep. She had to know that.

But then again, she *was* Jillian. And who could ever really know what went on in that mind of hers? Also, who could say how long it was going to take her to face reality and come back inside?

Muttering a few more choice expletives, he went over and shut the door. Then he stuck another log in the wood-burning half of the kitchen stove and stood in front of the heater in the living area until the place began to warm up again.

He'd just settled back into his chair and picked up his book when Jillian blew in again. She went straight to the heater and stood in front of it for three or four minutes, shivering and rubbing her hands together.

Eventually, when she was more or less thawed out, she went looking for the cat.

"Missy," she called softly. "Come on, sweetie...."

She tried the old iron bed in the corner first, where the cat had run to hide after the tail-crushing incident. He could have told her that most likely it wasn't under there, that the last time he'd seen it, it had been shooting off in the direction of the bathroom and the door to the stairs. But if he told her about the cat taking off into the kitchen, she might ask how he, who made a point of paying zero attention to the animal, had even noticed that dear little Missy was on the move. When he answered that one, she'd only start shouting at him again. He could do without more of her shouting.

She got down on her hands and knees and peered under the couch. When she stood again, she made a big deal of clearing her throat.

"What?"

"Missy's not under the couch."

"So?"

"Last night, I saw her coming out of your room. Maybe she's in there now. Do you mind if I…?" She let her voice trail off and gestured at the curtain that led to his bedroom.

"Be my guest." He was already looking down at his book again.

Jilly stared at the top of his bent head, thinking that, really, his very existence annoyed her. She had a distinct and quite powerful urge to say something rude. Somehow, she quelled it. She stepped past him and went through the curtain.

What she saw on the other side made her stomach turn over and the tiny hairs rise on the back of her neck.

Chapter 6

The room was the room of her dream. Everything—all of it—was just as she remembered it, from the ladder-back rocker under the window to the big dark dresser against the far wall, the one with the yellowed runner on top and the streaked mirror above. Jilly could see herself in that mirror. She looked as if she'd seen a ghost.

And maybe she had.

Her legs felt shaky. It would probably be a good idea if she sat down. The bed—honest-to-Pete, the same bed as in her dream, with the same dark headboard and faded patchwork quilt—was only a few feet away. She staggered over to it and dropped to the edge.

She still had her coat and hat on. And it was a good thing, too, because suddenly she was freezing again. She wrapped her arms around herself and hunched her shoulders and waited for the shivering to pass.

It did, fairly quickly, thank goodness. She took off her hat, wincing when she bumped the knot on her forehead.

Wait a minute. Gingerly, she touched the injury again. She *had* been knocked out last night. Maybe she'd suffered a minor loss of memory. Didn't people often lose short-term memory after a head injury bad enough to cause unconsciousness?

Yes. Of course. It was all starting to make sense now.

She'd come into this room last night, at some point—maybe doing just what she was doing now, looking for Missy. Then she'd been hit on the head and forgotten all about it. Then, last night, while she was sleeping, the memory had resurfaced and been incorporated into her dream.

It made perfect sense.

Jilly put her hat back on. "Missy?" she called.

She got no response. She looked under the dresser, under the bed, in the crude closet that had been constructed of two-by-fours braced against a wall and hung with more curtains made of that palm-tree-patterned fabric.

When she went back out to the living area, Will glanced up.

"No luck," she told him and then couldn't stop herself from asking, "By any chance, was I in your bedroom last night?"

Now he was looking at her as if she had several screws loose. Not, she reminded herself, that such a look from him was anything all that new or different. "Why the hell would you have been in my bedroom?"

"You know, I was asking myself the same question."

"And what kind of answer did you have for yourself?"

She wondered, Why am I talking to him? It always turns out badly when I do. "I have to tell you, I think this is a subject best not pursued."

"Then why did you bring it up?"

"Now *that's* a good question. Am I going to answer it? I think I'd rather not. I left my car running and I have to find my cat."

He grunted and went back to reading his book.

She realized she needed a little help from him. How unpleasant. She cleared her throat. "Excuse me?"

He let out a big gusty breath. "What is it, Jillian?"

"I hate to put you out, but do you think you could keep an eye on the doorway to your bedroom? Make sure Missy doesn't go darting in there while I'm looking for her in the rest of the house?"

Will seriously considered telling her to forget the cat for now—forget the cat and go out and turn off her damn car, since they both knew she wasn't going anywhere. But that would only inspire more argument. Let her figure it out for herself. She'd have to come to grips with reality as soon as she actually tried to drive off, anyway. "Sure. I'll watch for the cat."

"Thank you," she sneered.

She wandered off, calling, "Missy, Missy, here sweetie, come on…" He heard her footsteps on the stairs. She called the cat as she went. She stayed up there for a while, poking around, calling intermittently, "Missy, baby…come on now, come on…"

She came back down. "Missy? Where are you?

Missy, here girl…" She went into the bathroom, still calling. Then he heard her in the kitchen, opening and closing cabinets.

She popped her head around the half-wall and caught his eye, lifting one of those thick eyebrows in an unspoken question.

"Haven't seen it," he said.

She went back upstairs, still calling. It seemed to him he could hear the worry creeping into her voice, becoming more pronounced every time she said the cat's name.

Her concern somehow turned out to be contagious. He was starting to wonder, too, where the damn cat might be, starting to think about how she'd left the door open, how he'd sent the cat flying, how he'd turned his back on the door for several minutes while he peeked out the window to see what she was up to.

And how it *was* Christmas. And at Christmas, if you hung around Will Bravo, bad things seemed to always happen….

She came back downstairs and went out the door, shutting it carefully behind her. He got up, went to the window and lifted the blind. She appeared from the side porch, hunched against the wind. She slogged out to her 4Runner, opened the driver's door and leaned in. The windshield wipers stopped. She pulled her head out and shut the door again.

When she got back inside, she went straight to the heater to warm herself. He was still standing by the window. She took off her hat and smoothed her hair. "I don't know what to do next." All the usual animosity was gone from her voice. "I can't imagine where she might be."

Will didn't like what he was feeling. Guilt. It tightened his gut and squeezed at his chest. He shouldn't have shoved the cat off his lap like that—not with the door wide open, anyway.

"Jillian…"

She made a questioning sound and those dark brows drew together.

"I, uh, probably should have said something earlier."

"About?"

"The last time you went out, before you came back to get the cat, you left the door open."

She laid a cold-reddened hand against her throat. "How…long was it open?"

He hated to see her look so damn stricken. And he could see it in those gorgeous gray eyes: She was blaming herself. He couldn't stand that. He liked it better when she was sniping at him, or chattering away like Martha Stewart on speed. It was going to be a relief, he realized, to tell her the truth. Then she could get mad at him, maybe yell at him and call him a few rude names. He could take that. He could take just about anything, if she would only stop looking so worried and scared.

"At least five minutes," he said. "Probably more."

"Oh, no."

"Yeah. And I—" But she wasn't sticking around for the worst part of his confession. She was already putting her hat back on, turning for the door. "Jillian, wait."

"I can't. I have to go look for her. She was a stray when I found her, but she's been an indoor cat since then. And she's never been in the wild, that I know of." She pulled open the door and a flurry of snow blew in, borne on a frozen gust of wind. "She won't know how to cope." She went out the door and pulled it shut behind her.

Will just stood there for several seconds, thinking that an outdoor search was an exercise in futility. If the cat had wandered out the door, it was more than likely a frozen cat by now—and if not, it *would* be frozen very soon. And in the meantime, who the hell could say where it might be hiding? It could be anywhere. And he wouldn't put it past Jilly to get herself lost in the woods looking for it.

Will switched from his moccasins to his boots. Then he grabbed his coat off the peg and went after her.

Luckily, she hadn't gotten far. He found her in the woodshed, which was maybe ten feet from the house in the opposite direction from the clearing where they'd parked their cars.

She turned when he came through the open door. "What are you doing out here?" Her breath plumed on the frozen air.

"I want to help."

She didn't argue, only wrapped her coat tighter around her and peered into the gloom. "I should have brought a flashlight."

The woodshed was the simplest sort of structure, a tin roof, a wooden frame and rough plank walls. The wind whistled through the cracks between the planks. For as long as Will could remember, there had always been a flashlight hanging on a big rusted nail to the left of the door. He'd put fresh batteries in it just the other day, as a matter of fact.

"Right here." He grabbed it and turned it on.

They scoured the shed, shining the light in every nook and cranny. There were a lot of those. The wood was stacked three logs deep at the far end of the shed. With slow care, Will ran the flashlight over the rows of logs. They checked out the tool area, examined the big box of rags in the corner, looked over the shelves stacked with dusty jars. He shone the light behind more boxes full of nails and screws.

No Missy.

Will followed Jillian back out into the storm, stopping to pull the door shut and hook the latch. They circled the outside of the shed, to no avail. They checked the perimeter of the house, the two porches and then out behind, where the emergency generator and the propane tank were buried well above their bases in snow. They went on, hoping to find places that a cat might crawl into.

But the snow covered everything, smooth and deep. Once they'd been around the house and the shed, Jillian trudged into the bushes that rimmed the clearing.

Will knew it was pointless to keep at it—that it had probably been pointless from the first—but he didn't have the heart to tell her, so he went with her. For a time, they wandered around in the brush, hunched against the cold, protected a little from the storm by the close-growing trees, as Jillian called the cat and got no answer but the howling of the wind.

Finally, she turned to him, hands in her pockets,

bright red nose poking out under the brim of her hat, "I want to check the cars before we go in."

They traipsed to the vehicles. She hauled open the driver's door of her 4Runner and climbed in there to look around, he assumed in the faint hope that Missy might have jumped in while she had the door open. She checked underneath, where she'd had to dig out to get her chains on. No luck either place. His vehicle was buried to the base of the bumper. No way any animal was hiding under there.

The storm had intensified as they searched. By the time they turned back toward the house, it was almost as bad as it had been the night before. Snow and wind buffeted them. The world was a swirling, freezing wall of whiteness.

Back inside, she headed straight for the stairs. She went up and came back down, then she went into the bathroom, and all through the kitchen, the living area and his bedroom, checking every corner one more time, calling forlornly, "Here, Missy. Here, girl…"

Will took off his coat and his boots and warmed up at the heater, waiting for her to stand in one place for a minute or two—at which time he would confess to her that her darling Missy's disappearance was all his fault.

His opportunity wasn't that long in coming. Once she'd gone through the house a second time, she came back to the coat rack by the door. She took off her hat and her coat and hung them up, then unlaced her boots and set them next to his. He stepped aside so she could have the heater to herself for a minute or two.

She took the spot he offered and informed him solemnly, "I'm sorry. I'm not leaving without her."

She wasn't leaving in any case, since they were snowed in. But he decided there was no point in beating her over the head with the facts. If she didn't want to face them, fine. She finally understood that she was stuck here, and that was what mattered.

He shrugged and tried again to tell her what he had done. "Jilly, I—"

She cut him off with a groan. "Oh, this is ridiculous." And then she surprised him by admitting the truth, after all. "As if I ever was leaving in the first place. We both know I wasn't. But I just *had* to make my big scene." She shivered and stared miserably down at her thick red socks. "I'll never forgive myself if I've ended up costing Missy her life."

"Jilly."

She looked up. "Yeah?"

"If the damn cat did run out, it's not your fault."

She scrunched up her nose at him. "Oh, I don't know what's happened to you in the past half hour. All at once, you're just a wonderful, wonderful guy."

He tried to look thunderous. "Don't count on it lasting."

And she actually smiled—though her eyes didn't. "I won't, I promise—and if Missy got out, it *was* my fault."

"No, it wasn't."

"Yes, it was."

"No."

"Will. I was the one who—"

"No. You were not the one. When you left the door

open, I should have gone right over and shut it. But I was angry and I figured you could close the damn door yourself."

"Makes sense to me. If our positions had been reversed, I probably would have done exactly the same thing. And if you'd been the one with a cat and your cat had run out—"

"You would have been at fault."

"Oh, please, Will. You're a lawyer. Get real. She's *my* cat and *I'm* responsible for her safety."

This wasn't going the way he had planned. The woman was giving him logic, something he'd never in a million years have expected from her. "There's more. The cat didn't run out. Not at first. It jumped on my lap. I gave it a whack."

Jillian flinched. "You whacked my cat?"

Had he? Whacked it? "Well, it was a good, solid shove, anyway. The animal went flying."

"And she ran out the door?"

"Not exactly. She ran into the kitchen."

"And?"

"Hell, I don't know. I got up to look out the window and see what was taking you so damn long out there, and then it got so cold in here, I gave up and shut the door myself, after all."

"But you never saw Missy run out."

"It's obvious she ran out while I had my back turned."

"No, it's not. The only thing that's obvious is that *I* left the door open."

"I could have closed it right away."

"We've been over that. You were mad and you weren't about to shut the door that I had left open."

What was it with him and this woman? They could argue over anything. They'd even argue over who got to take the blame. "Jillian. I left the door open and I shoved the cat off my lap."

"No. *I* left the door open."

"But I—"

"Will. Could we just not argue? Please?"

"I only want you to understand that—"

"Uh-uh. My understanding is not what you want. What you want is to take the blame. But I'm not going to let you have the blame, because you don't deserve it—not in this case, anyway.

"Oh, Will…" Her voice had gone soft, with a quaver in it. A single tear was sliding down her cheek. "I know you're no animal lover. But you wouldn't hurt Missy on purpose. Smashing her tail with your chair was an accident. And pushing her off your lap wouldn't have hurt her. It was my fault. I left the door open."

"Jilly—"

"There's no point in beating this subject to death. I'm feeling kind of low, and I think I'll just go upstairs for a while."

Chapter 7

Will let her go. He understood that she needed some time to herself.

In an hour or two, he figured, she'd come back downstairs. He was kind of out of practice at consoling people, but as soon as she came back down, he'd try to cheer her up. He knew where to look to find a few decks of cards and a couple of board games. They could play whatever she wanted to play. And he'd let her choose the radio station.

At lunchtime, she was still up there. And she was so damn quiet. He hadn't heard her moving around at all. That didn't seem normal—not for someone like Jilly, who'd almost gone around the bend last night when he'd made her lie still on the couch for an hour.

But he thought he knew how to bring her down. He

had a pretty good idea of her food preferences—and he'd watched her eat. She was a girl with a serious appetite. By now, she had to be good and hungry.

He heated up a big can of Chef Boyardee ravioli. When he put the food on the stove, he opened the door to the stairs good and wide so the smell would drift up to her.

She didn't come down.

Outside, it was still snowing—and still well below freezing. He kept telling himself she'd at least have to come down long enough to struggle out to her car and bring in her champagne, her various vegetables and that free-range organic turkey of hers. But she didn't.

At one-thirty, he decided he'd better do something about her groceries, since it was becoming all too clear that *she* wasn't planning to. He put on his boots and his jacket and struggled through the snow, trekking back and forth from her car until he'd brought in everything—every damn bag of Cheez Doodles, as well as all her other stuff—the rest of the food and the suitcases, the laptop, the boom box. He got it all. Except the cat supplies.

Will was a realist. The cat, he was certain, had gone to that big scratching post in the sky. After all, he thought bleakly as he put her precious perishables in the fridge, it *is* Christmas. In Will's experience, the worst things always happened at Christmas. Little Missy's disappearance and ultimate demise was just one more link in the chain of yuletide disasters Will Bravo had known.

He glanced at the ceiling, wondering what she could be doing up there so *quietly*. It just wasn't like her.

Then again, maybe she was taking a long nap. Sleep would be good for her. And she was bound to come down soon.

Around two-thirty, he heard her footsteps on the stairs. His spirits rose. He set his book aside—but then he heard the bathroom door close. He figured she'd come on in the living area in a minute or two. She didn't. When she came out of the bathroom, she went back up the stairs.

Three o'clock came and went. And four. And five.

At dinnertime, he pulled out all the stops and whipped up a double batch of Kraft macaroni and cheese. Caitlin, who in the past few months had seemed to mention Jillian every ten minutes or so, had told him that she'd seen Jilly eat two huge bowls of macaroni and cheese at the Highgrade one lunchtime when she was in town for a visit with Jane. The Highgrade was the saloon/café/gaming establishment his mother had owned since before he was born.

"That girl can eat," Caitlin had said. "She told me the mac and cheese at my place was the best—next to Kraft." Caitlin had laughed that low, provocative laugh of hers. "Does that sound like anyone you know, my sweet darlin'?" She'd given him a wink, false eyelashes swooping down and fluttering up again.

At the time, he couldn't have cared less that Jillian Diamond shared his fondness for Kraft macaroni and cheese, and he'd told Caitlin as much. But right now, the information could come in handy.

He had the door open to the stairs and he banged the utensils around more than he needed to, trying to get her attention. When the food was ready, he carried the full pan over and fanned the steam up the stairwell.

Then he listened, closely, for the sound of her moving around.

Nothing.

She'd been up there for nine hours—minus that one trip down to use the bathroom. He understood her need to mourn the loss of her cat. But nine hours of silence and stillness from someone like Jilly simply wasn't natural. He mounted one step and then another and then he paused to listen some more.

Still nothing. He didn't like it. It was just too damn quiet up there. And it was dark, too. She hadn't even bothered to turn on a light.

He couldn't take it anymore.

He got a big bowl, filled it with macaroni and cheese and stuck a spoon in it. Then he grabbed two bags of Cheez Doodles and quietly started upward into the darkness at the top of the stairs.

He found her lying on the bed in the room beyond the curtain, fully dressed—or so it appeared, though most of her body was covered by one of his grandmother's old afghans. In the moonlight, the skin of her cheek and throat had the luster of pearl. She'd curled herself up in a fetal press, facing the wall, her tan-and-gold hair—shadows and silver by moonlight—trailing onto the pillow.

On the far side of the bed was a snowdrift of discarded tissues. She lay very still.

Too still? A shiver of fear coursed through him.

But no. He couldn't believe that she would end it all because her cat had wandered outside in a blizzard. Not Jilly. She could drive a man nuts with her constant babbling and her unrealistic, overbearing enthusiasms, but basically, in her own unusual way, she was well-balanced and mentally sound. He would lay odds on that.

Then again, it *was* Christmas Eve. In his experience, at Christmastime, all bets were off.

He leaned in closer. She was breathing—the shallow, even breathing of sleep. He resisted the urge to grab her shoulder and give it a shake just to make certain she'd wake up. Of course, she'd wake up. It was only his own paranoia that had him imagining otherwise.

Taking extreme care to be silent, he set the bowl on the bedside table and tiptoed back the way he'd come, pausing at the low dresser to drop off the Cheez Doodles, trying his damnedest to keep the bags from crackling in the process. He was just about to duck back through the curtain when he heard the bedsprings creak behind him. There was a click—the bedside lamp. A soft glow filled the room.

"Will?"

He turned. She was already sitting up, raking her hand back through her sleep-tangled hair. She had marks from the bedspread pattern pressed into her right cheek and those fine eyes were red-rimmed and puffy-looking, with dark shadows beneath. The puffy eyes and the pile of tissues told it all. She'd been doing some serious crying—and quietly. That really got to him, that she would lie up here for hours, silently crying. It was so unlike the Jillian he thought he knew.

She spotted the bags he'd just set on the dresser, glanced over at the night table and saw the bowl of macaroni and cheese. "Oh," she said, her lower lip quivering, looking so sad and sweet and grateful it cut him to the core. "The two major food groups. Oh, thank you, Will."

"Will you eat?" he asked, more gruffly than he meant to.

Her stomach growled right then, loudly. She put her hand on it and a smile broke across her face. "I guess I'd better." She grabbed the bowl, scooped up a big spoonful—and stopped with the spoon halfway to her mouth. "Did you?"

"What?"

"Eat."

"No, but—"

She dropped the spoon back in the bowl, pushed the afghan to her feet and slid off the bed. "Come on. Let's go downstairs. I can splash a little cold water on my face and you can fill yourself a bowl and pour us two giant glasses of milk."

When they got to the bottom of the stairs, she saw her suitcases, waiting where he'd left them, not far from kitchen door. She gave him another of those heart-twisting smiles. "You brought in my bags. Thank you."

He felt absurdly pleased with himself. "I thought you

might be needing them. And you don't have to worry about that expensive fresh turkey."

"You didn't." She turned and pulled open the refrigerator door. "You did. You brought in—"

"Pretty much everything." Except the cat supplies, which he decided it would be wiser not to mention.

She shut the refrigerator door. "I know it's awful out there. Thank you. Again."

"No problem. Go wash up and let's eat."

They ate and cleaned up the dishes without saying much. But the silence was okay, companionable and relaxed.

"For your entertainment this evening," he announced as she was wiping the counter, "you get your choice of checkers or Scrabble. I also play a killer game of Go Fish."

She smiled again. "What about poker? I bet you're good at that."

"Five-card stud, seven-card draw, no-limit Texas hold 'em. You name it, I play it. I'm not as good as Cade—but nobody's as good as Cade." His baby brother made his living with a deck of cards. He'd won the World Championship of Poker at Binion's in Vegas a few years back and he had the gold bracelet to prove it.

She was looking at him sideways. "You are being so good to me, it's making me nervous."

"It's my goal to behave like a bona fide human being for as long as we're stuck here together."

"An honorable goal—and do you know what I'd like more than just about anything right now?"

"Name it."

She hitched a thumb toward the bathroom door. "A long soak in that big tub in there."

"Be my guest."

She was in the bathroom for over an hour. Will tried to read his book, but his mind kept straying to grisly images of potential disaster: a tub drowning, a blow-dryer electrocution…

When he finally heard the bathroom door open, he breathed a hefty sigh of relief. He heard her go up the stairs. Great. Now, at last, he'd be able to concentrate on his book.

He'd read about three interminable sentences when he realized he could smell that enticing perfume she always wore. He set the book aside and followed his nose into the bathroom, where it was warm and steamy and her scent was everywhere.

He stood in there, just smelling the air, for several seconds. Then, feeling vaguely foolish, he flipped on the faucet over the old concrete sinks and washed his hands, knowing he was only doing it so he could tell himself he'd come in here for a valid reason, not just in order to smell Jilly Diamond's tempting perfume.

He dried his hands, pausing in the process to listen. Was she moving around up there? Was she really all right?

She'd seemed okay since he'd gone up the stairs to check on her. She'd even smiled now and then, and teased him about how nice he was being to her. She was fine, he was sure of it. He should just leave her alone.…

* * *

Jilly looked up from her laptop when she heard Will come up the stairs.

He stopped on the other side of the curtain. "Jilly?"

"I'm decent." She had on her fuzzy pajamas, which were modesty personified, as they covered more than most of the things she wore in the daytime. She'd pulled on a pair of thick yellow socks to keep her feet nice and toasty and she was sitting on top of the blankets, her computer in her lap. "Come on in."

He parted the curtain and stepped through. "Just checking on you." He looked incredibly handsome—and very concerned for her welfare.

A lovely, warm contented feeling flooded through her. "Well, let's see." She touched the bump on her head. "I think the danger of brain damage is past."

He gave her a gorgeous crooked smile. "I'm glad to hear it. But I was more thinking about…" He seemed at a loss for the most tactful way to phrase it.

"My emotional state?"

"Yeah."

"Let's say I'm a little wobbly, but at least I'm no longer curled in a ball sobbing my heart out."

"Sounds like progress."

"Oh, definitely." She indicated the clear space on the far side of the bed. "As you can see, I've dispensed with my mountain of used tissues. I won't be building another one."

"Very encouraging."

"Yes. I think so, too. And thanks for asking. For… caring."

"If there's anything else I can do, I want you to let me know."

She knew her next line. *Thanks so much, and have a nice night*.

But really, he didn't seem all that eager to get away. And while she didn't feel much like playing checkers, she wouldn't mind a little company for a while.

She picked up the open bag at her side and held it out. "Cheez Doodle? Hey, if you want to stick around for a while, I'll even turn off the Christmas music." It was one of her favorites, *Aaron Neville's Soulful Christmas*. "As you can see, I've already got it turned down very low in deference to your hatred of all things ho-ho-ho."

He folded those big arms and leaned against the pink Sheetrock doorframe. "I can hardly hear it."

"That's good?"

"It's fine." He was standing up straight again and coming her way. When he got to the bed, she handed him the bag. He took it and stood there, crunching away. "You're working?"

"Just a few notes for a column. I have to turn in five a week now. So I have to keep them coming."

"More advice to the lovelorn?"

She punched the Save icon and arched him a look. "Not at the moment." She closed the file and got out of the program.

"That's your column, right? Helping people work out their love lives?"

"I'll advise on anything—how to get stains out of your carpet, how to accessorize for success *and* how to pull yourself together after a failed love affair. There are those who say I have no shame when it comes to telling people how to live their lives. But I look at it this way. If the people ask, then I'll come up with an answer." She shut the laptop down. "Lately, I've been getting a lot of questions on holiday stress and how to handle it, so I'm working up something on that." She lowered the screen and slipped the computer to the floor, into the space between the lamp table and the bed.

There was nowhere else to sit except the bed and an uncomfortable-looking straight chair way over in the corner. She scooted sideways to make a space for him. He dropped down beside her, shucked off his moccasins and made himself comfortable, propping a pillow behind his back and leaning against the wall beneath the window. It looked as if he might be staying for a while.

Jilly decided that would be just fine with her. She plumped the pillow on her side and leaned back against it with a sigh. He held out the bag, she grabbed a handful. For a minute or two, they sat there, chewing, as Aaron Neville sang "White Christmas," the volume so low it almost seemed to Jilly that the music was only in her head.

She sent him a look.

"What?"

"Well, I can't help but wonder…"

He seemed a little wary, but not dangerously so. "Wonder what?"

"I guess I can just ask and you can tell me it's none of my business—but in a friendly way, okay?—if you don't want to answer."

He actually chuckled. "Go for it."

"Why do you hate Christmas?"

He grunted. "I guess I should have known that was coming."

"Oh, come on." She reached for the bag. He tipped it her way. She took another handful and popped three or four of the crunchy cheesy morsels into her mouth. "Just tell me. If you don't, I'll only ask Celia or Jane the next time I talk to them."

"You do that, huh? Talk to your friends about me?"

"I haven't up till now. Until now, I've been scrupulously careful never to ask my friends *anything* about you."

"Never?"

"That's what I said."

"Why *scrupulously?*"

"Oh, please. It's obvious."

"Tell me, anyway."

She knew what he was up to. "First, you tell me if you're going to answer *my* question."

"Jilly…"

"Well, are you?"

"The answer to your question is very long and very sad and once you hear it, you'll wish you hadn't asked."

"I'll be the judge of that."

He looked at her for a long time. Then he said, "Cute pajamas. I like the stripes. And the daisies."

"You are not even close to distracting me from my intent."

"I can't believe you've got me considering telling you."

"I'm a very charming woman, once you get used to me."

"Not to mention relentless."

"That, too. Will you tell me?"

"If I do, you have to remember that you asked for it—and kept asking for it—until I gave in."

"Agreed."

He looked at her again—a long, deep look. And for just a second or two, in spite of the fact that he was a young, broad-shouldered, healthy-looking man, she saw a flash of resemblance to the frail old woman in her dream of the night before. It occurred to her that she'd never seen Mavis McCormack—in the flesh or in a photograph. And she couldn't help wondering about the woman in her dream. Did she look even remotely like the real Mavis?

"Have you got a picture of your grandmother around here anywhere?"

He blinked. "Did the subject just change again, or am I imagining things?"

She laughed. "Sorry. I do that. My boss at the *Press-Telegram* calls me the queen of the non sequitur. I think it's something to do with the creative mindset."

"Ah."

"And about that picture?"

He shrugged. "There's a bunch of stuff in boxes and trunks stuck in the crawl space behind that closet." He gestured at another makeshift curtained affair in the corner, similar to the one downstairs. "I'm pretty sure there are some old photographs of her in there. We can look tomorrow, since I'd venture a guess we won't be going anywhere."

"Oh, I would love that. Who knows what we might find?"

"And are you going to tell me why you've suddenly got to see a picture of my Grandma Mavis?"

She thought of her dream—of the two of them, naked and glowing, floating in a soft, warm void, making mad, wonderful, passionate love. No way was she getting into that with him. "Just wondering about her. I mean, this *was* her house...."

He didn't speak for a moment. Jilly couldn't guess what he might be thinking. Then he said, "People said she was crazy, but she wasn't. She was shy, really. Nervous around strangers. Liked to keep to herself. She lived up here, in this house, all alone, for most of her life. She raised my mother up here."

She couldn't resist asking, "What about your grandfather? Where does he fit into the picture?"

He lifted an eyebrow at her. "He doesn't—not in my lifetime, anyway. And not in Ma's either, as far as I know."

"Caitlin never knew her father?"

"That's right. And it's likely that my grandmother didn't know him for very long. McCormack *was* her maiden name. Whoever he was, he hung around long enough to get my grandmother pregnant with Caitlin and then vanished without ever bothering to come up with a wedding band—but you know that, don't you?"

She gave him a half shrug. Of course she knew. They both came from the same hometown, after all. And in

New Venice, Mad Mavis and Caitlin and her three wild sons had always been the topic of gossip and conjecture. People loved to whisper about how Mad Mavis McCormack had Caitlin up in that old house of hers, all alone, without getting married first—without even any evidence of a man in her life.

Will made a low noise in his throat. "Around the Highgrade they always joked about it, called it Mad Mavis's immaculate conception. They said that Caitlin was a product of a virgin birth. The drunks got a good laugh over that one, considering the way Caitlin turned out."

Jilly took his meaning. Caitlin McCormack Bravo was about as far from a virgin as any woman could get. By the time she was twenty-one, she'd had two sons, Aaron and Will, by the notorious Blake Bravo—and she was pregnant with Cade. Blake had then disappeared, by faking his own death, as it turned out. He'd never been seen by anyone in New Venice again. And after that, for Caitlin, there had been an endless string of affairs. The men seemed to get younger as Caitlin matured. Her last boyfriend had been around the same age as her sons.

Jilly said softly, "You were close to her, to Mavis, weren't you?"

Will was looking off toward the pineapple-adorned curtain, a musing expression on his face. "I remember her as gentle. And that she was good to me. Ma always said I was her favorite. I don't know if that's true. But in the summer sometimes, I used to stay up here with her, just the two of us. We didn't talk much. We played checkers and Scrabble and I always felt…at peace with myself here."

"When did she die?"

"Twenty years ago yesterday."

Jilly felt a coldness, like a drop of icy water slithering down her spine. She'd dreamed of Mad Mavis on the twenty-year anniversary of the woman's death.

Just a coincidence, she hastened to tell herself. And surely it was. But that didn't make it any less unsettling.

She asked, "So that's the reason you hate Christmas? Because the grandmother you loved died on December twenty-third?"

He slanted her a look. "Uh-uh. First, you tell me why you think you have to make a point of not talking about me to your friends."

"Oh, Will. Come on. You can figure it out."

"Tell me anyway."

"Because I don't want them thinking I've got a thing for you." She said it, and then couldn't quite believe that she had.

She just knew he was going to ask, Have *you got a thing for me?* What she wasn't sure about was how she would answer him. Now he was being so kind, making an effort, as he'd put it, *to behave like a bona fide human being,* she couldn't help starting to find him attractive all over again.

But he didn't ask. He only said, with a sincerity that melted her heart, "I'm damn sorry about the rotten things you heard me say that night at Jane's. I'm not going to make any excuses for myself. There are none.

But it wasn't really about you. You know that, don't you?"

"Yeah. I guess I do."

"You're an attractive woman. You're smart. You're fun to be around. And you *are* charming—too damn charming, in fact, for my peace of mind."

"I am?"

"Absolutely. Maybe that's why I've been so hard on you. To keep you at a distance." Oh, my. She was certainly liking the sound of this. And then he added, "You're something special, Jilly Diamond."

And she realized she was glad she'd come here, in spite of everything, in spite of how mean he'd been earlier, in spite of a big tree limb dropping on her head, in spite of having some kind of visitation from a dead old lady in the middle of the night, in spite of all of it—well, except for Missy's disappearance. She really could have done without that.

"It's just that I'm…" He seemed to be seeking the right words.

She thought maybe she had them. "Not in the market?"

"Yeah. That's it. I'm not in the market—though, when I look at you, I could almost wish I was."

Her throat had gone dry. From the Cheez Doodles, of course. She swallowed.

"Want a root beer?" Will was already swinging his feet to the floor. "I think we really need a root beer." He slid on his moccasins and stood, pausing to hand her the bag before he turned for the curtain.

"Will."

He stopped and looked back at her.

"I haven't forgotten and you're not getting off the hook."

He shook his head. "You really don't want to hear it."

"Yes, I do. I want to hear all of it, the whole long, sad story."

He suggested ruefully, "We could just play checkers."

"Not on your life."

Chapter 8

"It started when I was little." Will settled back against the pillow and popped the top on his root beer. "My earliest memories of Christmas are depressing ones. Looking back, I don't know how Caitlin managed—three boys to raise, a business to run and my father long gone before Cade was even born. I think, given all she had on her plate, she did a damn fine job. But we had some seriously lean years there at first."

Outside, the wind was up again, making the pines cry. Jilly glanced over her shoulder as a particularly hard gust shook the windowpane behind them. She thought of Missy, all alone out there, and sadness squeezed her heart.

Will was watching her. "You okay?"

She nodded. "Please. Go on."

"Jilly—"

"No. I want you to. I do. You had some seriously lean years…"

After a moment, he continued. "When you're a kid, you don't think of how your mom is killing herself to make a life for you and your brothers. You think, why aren't we like all the other families in town? I didn't get it, you know?"

"You just said it. You were little."

He grunted. "I was little, and I was resentful. Somehow, even from the first, Caitlin always managed to hang a few strands of tinsel downstairs in the High-grade. She'd stencil grinning snowmen and happy Santas in the windows. She and Bertha—you know Bertha?"

"Of course." Bertha Slider was a big, good-natured woman with freckles and carrot-red hair. She'd been Caitlin's second-in-command at the Highgrade for as long as Jilly could remember.

"Well, Ma and Bertha would put up a tree in the corner of the bar. But Caitlin just didn't seem to have the time or energy left over to get us a tree for our apartment upstairs. Christmas Eve, she'd work the bar, serving up the good cheer to all the sad and lonely types who had nowhere else to go for the holidays. She was always good behind the bar, you know? It's one of the secrets of her ultimate success."

Jilly did know. "She can be so exasperating. But what a heart."

"Yeah. A lot of running a bar is about being ready with a sympathetic ear and a shoulder to cry on. And Christmas Eve, her shoulder would get a major workout.

She wouldn't drag herself up to bed until after three or four sometimes. Christmas morning, she'd sleep late. Not that it mattered. There was no tree in the first place and nothing much to put under it, if there had been."

"Pretty bleak," Jilly said.

"From the viewpoint of a seven- or eight-year-old kid, you bet it was. I look back now, I can see she was knocking herself out to make a life for us. But at the time, all I saw was that she wasn't like other moms, that we had no dad. And the only Christmas around our place was down in the bar."

"So what about Cade and Aaron? Do they hate Christmas, too?"

"Not that I know of. I wouldn't say they're exactly crazy about the holiday season, but they've always seemed pretty much okay with it, as far as I could see."

"So what makes you different?"

"Maybe it's partly that my birthday is December twenty-sixth."

"Eeeuu. Tough."

"I wouldn't call it the end of the world. It only seemed like it at the time. If somehow Caitlin managed to provide some kind of Christmas, no way she had the energy to make a big deal over me the next day."

"You never had a cake? Or presents?"

"Sometimes. And sometimes everyone would just forget about it—well, except for Grandma Mavis. She would always have something for me for my birthday. She didn't come down into town a lot. Sometimes I wouldn't see her till weeks later. But when I did see her, she'd have something all wrapped for me and it would make me feel good. But a lot of times, on my birthday itself, I'd get nothing—and by nothing, I don't mean so much the cake and the presents. I mean the attention. The right kind of attention, the kind that tells a kid people are glad he's around, happy he was born. On my birthday, as a rule, I either felt forgotten, or I felt like just one more burden, one more job on Caitlin's endless to-do list."

Jilly was nodding. "Bleaker than bleak."

"But on the plus side, it did get better."

"As the years went by?"

"Yeah. When I was nine, I got a cake *and* a puppy. God, I was happy. I'd been asking for a dog for about three years by then. And I finally got one. He was a lab-and-shepherd mix and he was the sweetest damn dog that ever was. I was crazy about him."

"Why do I think there's a grim punch line coming?"

"Probably because he was run over and killed two days before my twelfth birthday—on Christmas Eve. Run over and killed by a drunk driver in the parking lot behind the Highgrade."

Jilly let out a sympathetic moan. "Oh, Will. I'm so sorry."

"Pitiful, isn't it? And then, two years later, Ma finally coaxed Grandma Mavis into visiting us for Christmas. By then, well, you know how we were, my brothers and I. Wild, to put it mildly. Cade and Aaron were off God knows where. But I stuck close to home that year, to be with Grandma. I tried to be cool about it, but I was so damn excited that she was there. I knew she'd make Christmas special, and I knew that she'd fuss over me on my birthday, too. She had this old rattletrap Ford pickup and she and I went out together two days before Christmas to cut down a tree."

"Oh, I don't like the sound of this. Two days before Christmas would be the twenty-third. And the twenty-third of December was the day that she—"

"Who's telling this story?"

"Oops. Sorry."

"I remember how happy I was, this kind of glowing feeling I had, to be with her. We got the tree and we drove back to town. She parked in one of the spaces right by the back door of the Highgrade and she turned to me..." His voice trailed off. He sipped from his root beer before he went on. "That was when I realized something was wrong. She looked so old, I remember thinking. The wrinkles in her face looked deeper than ever before. And the skin around her mouth was dead white. I asked her what was wrong. She forced a smile and said she was a little tired. She thought maybe she'd go on upstairs and lie down...."

Outside, the wind, for a moment, had died. The final Christmas tune had played a few minutes before and the boom box was silent. The room seemed, at that moment, supernaturally quiet.

Jilly heard herself whisper, "Oh, no..."

Will said, "What I wanted, more than anything right then, was to believe her. I wanted it to be like she said. That she was just tired and a little rest would make everything better. I helped her up the stairs. She stretched out on the sofa in the living room. She said, 'Yes. Now that is much better.' I said, 'Grandma, maybe I oughtta go and get Ma, don't you think?' She waved her hand at me. She said again that she was fine. She said she wanted me to put up the tree, there by the window, so she could see it. She did seem better, I told myself. A little rest, and she would be fine. I got out the tree stand and put it by the window and went down and got the tree myself and hauled it up the stairs. I was so damn proud to have managed it all on my own. I got it on the stand and I stood back to look at it. I remember what I said. 'So Grandma. Looks good, don't you think?' She didn't answer."

"She was gone?"

"That's right."

"Oh, I need a Kleenex and I hate this story."

The box was on the night table. He passed it to her. Jilly yanked out a tissue. "Here. Hold this." She pushed her root beer at him. He set the box on the bed between them, next to the bag of Cheez Doodles, and took the can from her. She blew her nose and then demanded, "You blame yourself, don't you?"

He gave the root beer back to her. "I tell myself that she insisted she was all right—that I was a kid and I desperately wanted to believe what she said. That she had a massive heart attack and there was probably nothing anyone could have done for her, anyway."

"But you still blame yourself."

He leaned close, a sad smile on that wonderful mouth and a teasing look in those blue, blue eyes. "Tell you what."

She dabbed at her eyes. "What?"

"Just say the word. I'll get the checkers."

She waved her wadded-up Kleenex at him. "Uh-uh. No way. Tell the rest."

"Jilly—"

"I mean it. I want to hear the rest."

He settled back on his pillow. "Well, let's see…" He shot her a look. "Remember, you asked for this."

"Come on, what next?"

"Next, there was Mitzi Overposter. I think of Mitzi as just more of the same."

"Wait a minute. I know Mitzi. She still lives in New Venice."

He saluted her with his root-beer can. "That's right. Married to Monty Lipcott, with four kids last I heard— Monty junior and three little girls. Monty senior sells insurance now. But back then, he was New Venice High's star quarterback."

"Are you saying Mitzi dumped you for Monty?"

"You got it. I realize now she was not the love of my life, but it certainly felt like she was at the time. I caught her with Monty at Devon Millay's Christmas party. They were making out in the walk-in closet in Devon's mother's bedroom—well, more than making out. It's just possible I witnessed Monty junior's conception. I remember that when I pulled open that closet door, 'Jingle Bells' was playing on the stereo in the living room." Will drained the last of his root beer. "Where's the wastebasket?"

"Over here, on my side." She held out her hand and he passed her the empty can. She got rid of it, along with her own can and her used tissue. "So after Mitzi, you—"

Right then, everything went black.

"Oh, no," Jilly groaned.

Will's voice came at her, disembodied, through the darkness. "It was bound to happen sooner or later, with the storm this bad. I was surprised it stayed on all last night." The bedsprings complained as he shifted his weight. "A few years ago, I put in a generator for situations like this."

"I saw it, on the back side of the house, knee-deep in snow."

"Which is why I don't want to deal with it tonight."

"Smart thinking."

"I'll just get some candles." He was standing by then. She could see nothing, but she'd felt him leave the bed and his voice came from above.

"I'll go with you."

"No need." He was already moving away. She heard his soft tread as he crossed to the dresser. He opened a drawer. A second or two later, a flashlight's beam cut the darkness. "I'll be right back."

When he returned he had a box of votives and a stack of saucers. She helped him put the candles around, several on the dresser, a couple on the night table. They lit them.

"Okay, now," she said when they had stretched out on the bed again. "Tell me the rest."

He laughed. "I think I've told you enough—way more than enough."

"Uh-uh. You haven't. Not near enough."

"Hell, Jilly."

"Please?"

"I'll say this. After Mitzi, I decided I was too young

to get serious over a girl. So I didn't. For more than decade."

"But then?" She waited, half expecting him to back out of telling the rest.

But he didn't. "Five and a half years ago, I met Nora Talbot. And I knew, the first second I saw her, that I would love her. The miracle was, she felt the same way. I asked her to marry me and she said yes. We'd met in February, so we settled on Valentine's Day, which was a few days short of one year from when we met, for the wedding. But the wedding never happened. She was murdered when she stopped at an ATM to pick up some cash. Shot through the head by a two-bit thug who is waiting his turn on death row as we speak, I am pleased to say. It was Christmas Day."

"Oh God, Will. That's terrible. I am so sorry."

He'd been looking off toward the curtain, his profile rimmed in gold from the candlelight, but now he turned to her. "Why do people always say that, 'I'm sorry,' like it's their fault somehow?" His voice was harsh, his face shadowed.

She didn't shrink from him. "I guess because there's nothing else to say. It's not about whose fault it is. It's about regret. About how we wish it could have been different, that your Nora had lived, that you'd had a beautiful Valentine's Day wedding, that—"

"Never mind." His voice had gentled. "I get your point—and now I think it's your turn."

She almost opened her mouth to say something coy— *Oh, we're taking turns, are we?*—but then she thought of all that he had told her, especially the story of how his grandmother had died and the sad, bare facts about what had happened to Nora. Being coy just wasn't going to cut it. She shivered.

"Cold?"

"A little." She was already scooting down, reaching for the afghan.

He helped her, smoothing it over her, tucking it in around her. "Better?"

"Um-hm." She was thinking that he smelled good, that she could feel his body's warmth.

Oh-so-gently, he brushed the hair back from the bump at her temple. "Still hurting?"

She looked up at his shadowed face and thought of her dream, of Mavis, at the end, tucking her in. And then of the rest of it, of the way he had kissed her. That still remained so vivid, somehow, the power in his kiss....

"Jilly?"

The bump on her head. He had asked how it was. "I'd forgotten all about it until you asked."

"Not hurting, then?"

"Not in the least."

He rolled away from her and stood.

"You're leaving?" She hoped she didn't sound as forlorn as she felt.

"I was just going to get another blanket. But if you want to be left alone...?"

"I don't. I'd rather have company. It keeps my mind off worrying about Missy."

"Okay, then."

With a contented little sigh, she snuggled down and watched him pad in stocking feet over to the dresser.

Pure self-indulgence, Bravo, Will was thinking as he pulled open the bottom drawer and got the spare afghan.

Pure self-indulgence to be here in the candlelight with Jilly now. He ought to be ashamed of himself. Supposedly, he'd come up here to make sure she was all right.

She was fine. So what was he doing, lying on her bed with her, rambling on and on about himself? Just what she needed, after all she'd been through since having the misfortune to be snowed in with him—a chance to hear his long, sad story: Nightmare Christmases I Have Known.

He should go.

But he didn't go. He returned to the bed, stretched out next to her again and settled the blanket over himself.

When he turned to her, those fine gray eyes of hers were soft with understanding. "So you've got issues. Pet issues. Falling-in-love issues. And most definitely Christmas issues."

He really would have liked to disagree with her assessment. However, at that point, after spilling his guts so thoroughly, she couldn't help but peg any denials as outright lies. "You're right, I guess. At least about the pets."

"Oh, right." She let out an exaggerated groan. "Just the pets."

"Hey, I'll admit it. I haven't had a pet since Snatch got his in the Highgrade parking lot."

Her eyes went wide. Even in the warm glow of the candles, he could see that her face had paled.

"What's the matter?"

She blinked. "Nothing. Not a thing."

He didn't buy that for an instant. "Come on. What is it?"

"Really. Nothing."

"Are you sure?"

"Positive."

He wanted to probe further, but the look of shock he'd seen on her face was gone. Whatever he'd said that had rattled her, she'd pulled herself together now. She looked...purposeful. "Let's talk about the Christmas issues, shall we?"

"Let's not."

"You blame yourself for your grandmother's death—which happened at Christmas. You haven't had a pet since your dog, Snatch, died—at Christmas. You're hopelessly scared something awful will happen to you, or someone close to you, when it's Christmas. I'd imagine Nora's death was the final straw. Since you lost her, you hole up here, all alone, and wait the holiday out. You're not willing to try again—to have yourself a decent Christmas, to care for a pet, or to get something going with a woman. You're afraid what happened before will just happen again, that you'll lose what you love. And you're certain that when it does happen, it's going to be at Christmas and you irrationally tell yourself that—"

"Jilly."

"What?"

"You can stop now. You nailed me."

A big, beautiful smile bloomed on that wide mouth of hers. "I did, didn't I?"

"And now, it's time we moved on."

"To?"

"Don't give me that look. I'm not buying."

She groaned. "Oh, Will. You don't need to hear it."

"That's right. I don't. But I want to. And fair's fair. Don't give me any lightweight stuff."

"What does that mean?"

"It means I don't want to know what your sign is. I don't want to know your favorite color or if you prefer jazz or hip-hop or punk. I want the dirt. I want the issues. That way, when we get out of here and we both show up at Jane and Cade's or Aaron and Celia's for some event or other, I'll have as much on you as you have on me."

She let out a loud bark of delighted laughter. He'd always liked that about her, how when she laughed, she really went for it. "Will. You are terrifying."

"No. I'm a lawyer with personal issues, and *that* is terrifying." He realized he was having a very good time. Maybe too good a time.

She craned her head toward him, squinting.

God, she smelled good. He pulled back. "What?"

"You were smiling, and then you stopped smiling. But the light's behind you. It's hard to see your expressions clearly."

"You're evading."

She knew exactly what he was up to. "*Who's* evading?"

"Jilly, we've done me. Now, we're doing you."

"Oh, all right." She huffed and puffed a little, to show him how unnecessary she thought it was to tell him about herself. Then, at last, she said, "I have a job I love—in spite of how *some* people think that what I do is silly."

"Some people are idiots—and remember, this is about you, not me. And since your job is not an issue, that's enough about your job."

"You are so demanding."

"Issues, Jilly. Issues."

She blew out another huffy breath. "I honestly don't have a lot of them. Nothing earth-shattering, you know? I had a nice, secure childhood. My parents are still married—to each other. I've got two sisters, one older and one younger. They're both happily married and they both have kids."

"And you're not."

"That's right. I'm not married and I don't have kids. However, I *am* happy."

"But your mom and your sisters are always after you. They think you should find a good man, settle down, have a baby."

"Think you're pretty smart, don't you?"

"Would that be a yes?"

"Okay, it would."

"So *is* that what you want, then? To be married, with children?"

"Eventually, yes. Maybe."

"That was an answer?"

"Oh, Will. If the right guy came along tomorrow, who's to say? But if he doesn't, I'm just fine. It's the coupled-up nature of the world as we know it that gets to me. It just gets a little old, that's all. My mom and my sisters and their pitying looks. And now, my best friends are married, too. Celia's pregnant." Aaron's wife was very, very pregnant. Every time Will saw her lately, he felt certain she'd be going into labor any minute now. "Jane's trying to *get* pregnant. Everybody's half of a couple, and all the women are reproducing."

"You feel left out?"

"At times." She frowned. "But does it amount to an issue? Not really. The truth is, I'm happy just as I am. I'd like someone special in my life, yes. But marriage? I'm not even sure if I'm ready for it. I certainly wasn't the first time around."

He'd heard from Caitlin that there was an ex, so that information didn't surprise him. As a matter of fact, he'd been waiting for her to volunteer it. "Now, we're getting somewhere. You're divorced."

"I was twenty-two. Benny was twenty-nine. I thought it was a love for all time. It turned out to be a love for about fifteen minutes. Benny sold time-shares. He was good at it, too. He was already a millionaire, at least on paper, when we got together. Benny was everyone's best friend. Especially if she was young and good-looking. Jane spotted him for a runaround the first time she met him."

"Just by looking at him?"

"He made a pass at her."

"Ow."

"Yeah. She tried to tell me. But I only got mad at her. I thought she was being jealous and spiteful, after the way her marriage had turned out." Jane's first husband had been a born loser. He'd ended up dead early on, and from what Will had heard, he'd deserved what he got. Jilly said, "I didn't speak to her for months after she dared to inform me that my darling Benny had put the moves on her."

"And then?"

"Oh, it's so classic. I walked in on him with someone else. In *our* bed. I divorced him and gave the bed to the Salvation Army. So much for a love for all time."

"I hope you got yourself a huge divorce settlement."

"I probably should have. But I was young and foolish, with a broken heart. All I wanted was out. He was happy to oblige me, since I didn't ask for any of his money." She yawned. "So okay. Is that enough with the issues for now?"

By that time, they were both good and cozy, lying on their sides, face-to-face, pillows tucked beneath their heads.

Time to get up and say goodnight, Will told himself. But he didn't move. It was nice there, in the candlelight. And the storm seemed to have abated a little. The wind no longer cried through the pines or rattled the windows. The snow was still falling, though.

Jilly whispered, "Hear that? No wind, and the snow still coming down. Oh, I love that sound. That soft, soft sound. A kind of hushed sound, you know, with a tiny crackling to it?"

He made a low noise, agreeing with her.

"It's so peaceful...."

"Yeah."

For a while, they just lay there in the candlelight, wrapped up in their separate afghans, the empty Cheez Doodles bag between them, listening to the quiet sound of snow falling through a windless night.

Will watched as Jilly's dark, thick eyelashes fluttered down. He studied her face. Good, high cheekbones and a very strong chin, that wide mouth and those dark lashes and brows. And a large purple lump on her right temple.

He smiled to himself. She insisted it was all right. He supposed she knew what she was talking about. If that bump was going to give her any problems, there would have been indications by now.

He wanted to reach out and smooth her hair back, ask her if she was feeling any pain at all. But he'd already done that once. If he did it again, she was bound to figure out that he was just using her welfare as an excuse to put his hand on her.

He liked putting his hand on her. He would very much enjoy putting his hand on a lot more than the bump on her head. And now that her continued proximity had forced him to let down his guard and admit that he found her damned attractive, he had to be careful. Or he'd do what came naturally and make a serious move on her.

Yeah, all right. He wanted her. He was willing to cop to that—he *had* copped to it. But he really wasn't up for any lifetime commitment. And it just seemed like a bad idea, to get into something hot, heavy and temporary with a woman who confided in the women who were married to his brothers.

And anyway, who was to say Jilly would even be

interested in anything hot and heavy with him—temporary or otherwise? Yes, at one time he'd thought she might be attracted. But he'd taken care of that two weeks ago by opening his mouth and firmly inserting his foot while she just happened to be standing within earshot.

Tonight, they'd come a long way toward mending the breach. But it was a friend thing with her now. Wasn't it?

He should go.

But her face had softened, her lips had parted slightly. She'd fallen asleep. If he got up, the creaking and shifting of the old mattress would probably wake her.

And he felt so comfortable, lying here in the quiet with her.

Will closed his eyes.

Jilly woke to an icy wind blowing through the room. Her eyes popped open and she gasped as the candles, down to mere puddles of wax now, guttered and went out. The mysterious wind died instantly, as if it had only been the cold breath of a merciless giant, intent on putting out the lights.

Alarmed and disoriented, Jilly lay utterly still, the afghan pulled up close to her ears, staring wide-eyed at Will, who was sound asleep on the other pillow. Outside, it was still snowing. She could hear it whispering down. As her eyes adjusted, she could see Will's face more clearly. He looked so peaceful and relaxed.

She dared to squirm a little under her afghan, half expecting something awful to happen because she had moved. But nothing did.

And Will was still lying there, totally oblivious to whatever was going on. She hated to wake him, but that wind thing had just been a little too weird.

She whispered, "Hey. Will."

He didn't move, didn't so much as sigh.

"Will. Yoo-hoo. Wake up." Nothing. She pushed her afghan aside just enough that she could reach across and shake him. But when she tried to grab his shoulder, her hand went right through it.

Jilly gulped. "Oh, great." She grabbed the edge of the afghan and hauled it over her head. It smelled of mothballs. She didn't care what it smelled like. She was keeping it over her head. No way was she going to look and see if anyone happened to be standing—or hovering—at the end of the bed. She was going back to sleep and when she woke up again it would be real life and it would be morning.

She closed her eyes. "Sleep. I'm going to sleep. I am feeling very, very sleepy…."

Oh yeah, right.

Her eyes popped open again.

"One peek. That's all. I will check and make sure she isn't there and as soon as I do that, I'll be able to sleep again." Jilly edged back the afghan and lifted her head just enough to see over the empty Cheez Doodles bag.

And there was Mavis, floating at the foot of the bed, her blue eyes sad and knowing, her skinny arm outstretched.

Chapter 9

Jilly sat up. "Okay, Mavis. I've got to hand it to you. That bit with the dog? Inspired. I actually believe now that something really is happening here. What, I'm not quite sure. But something, I'll give you that. However, whatever it is, I don't think I like it. So how about if I just say, no thank you, I don't want to go with you now, I don't want to see whatever it is you've got to show me tonight? How would that be?"

Mavis smiled, her pretty teeth gleaming through the darkness, the wrinkles on her winter apple of a face growing deeper, more pronounced as the corners of her mouth stretched wide.

"Yes? Are you telling me yes?"

Mavis shook her head.

Surely there had to be some way to get through to

her. "Look. I know he's your favorite grandson and you love him and your spirit is troubled because he's never found happiness—or when he did, he lost it way too soon." Thinking about Will and how he had suffered, Jilly realized she had a thing or two to say to the apparition before her. "You know, Mavis? As long as you're hovering there, I would like to make one teensy little point."

Mavis continued floating, looking sad, arm outstretched.

Jilly laid it on her. "How could you die right in front of him like that? He was just a boy and it broke his heart. Why couldn't you at least let him run and get Caitlin, let him do what he could to save you?"

Mavis didn't answer. She stared and she floated and she held out her hand.

"And Mavis, as far as my making dream-love with Will, I think it's a bad idea. I don't want to do it again. Please don't try and tempt me. Because I won't." Did she sound firm enough? Oh, she hoped so. Because when she thought of Will's imaginary kiss, she got that dangerous quivery feeling in her stomach. She stuck out her chin and tried to look unbudgeable. "Got it?"

Mavis didn't speak, blink, smile or frown. She simply began floating toward Jilly through the bed, just like the night before.

Jilly sighed. "I guess there's no way to get out of this, is there?"

That skinny, wrinkled hand was right there, waiting. Jilly gave in and took it.

* * *

When the walls reformed again, they were outside, in the woodshed.

Jilly groaned. She knew what would happen next: Will, in the woodpile, without a stitch on, beckoning.

"Oh no," Jilly grumbled. "Mavis. Please. Not out here. Not in the woodshed."

Mavis's skinny finger pointed. But not toward the woodpile, toward the rag box in the corner.

"What? By that box? Nope. Sorry. I don't see him."

Mavis only kept pointing.

Jilly floated over and looked in the box, expecting to see a miniature Will, anatomically correct and pleading in a chipmunk voice, "Help me out, Jilly. Help me out, please."

But it wasn't Will. It was Missy.

Her own dear, sweet Missy. Curled in a ball and fast asleep among the rags.

Jilly opened her eyes. The sun shone in the window. The storm had passed at last.

"Omigod!" She bolted upright, pressed her palms together and cast her gaze heavenward. "Please, please, let it be true…"

"What the hell?" Will sat up. His hair stuck out in spikes and he had morning beard-shadow sprouting on that sexy cleft chin of his.

Jilly overflowed with fondness. She grabbed him and hugged him, hard. The empty snack bag, caught between them, crackled in protest as she squeezed.

"Wha…huh?" He was so adorable, so totally at a loss.

She laid her head against his broad chest and heard the strong, steady beat of his heart. "Will, I just know it. I just know that it's true."

"What? I don't get it. What's the—"

"Uh-uh." She beamed up into his frowning face as a single tear born of hope and joy slid down her cheek. "Not right now."

He saw the tear and rubbed it away with a gentle thumb. "Not right now, what?"

She pushed at his chest. "No time to explain." Windmilling her feet, she got them free of the hampering afghan. Then she threw herself at the end of the bed, scrambled off it and raced for the stairs, which she took two at a time, a neat trick, as the stairs were very steep and very narrow.

Will was right behind her. "What the—?"

"Oh, you'll see. Just wait. You'll see." She hit the kitchen floor at a run and raced to her boots, grabbing one and then the other, swiftly shoving her feet into them.

"I take it we're going outdoors." Will pulled on his own boots.

"Yep. But don't worry. We're not going far." She grabbed her coat and turned for the door.

Outside it was bright and utterly gorgeous, if you didn't mind blinding vistas of sparkling white. Jilly hustled to the end of the porch and then started trudging through the snow, which was several inches deeper than it had been last night. She hadn't laced her boots and the snow came to her knees. She hauled one leg up, shoved it down, and then repeated the process all over again.

The snow packed in over her open boot tops. It was cold on her feet as it melted with her body heat. Did she care?

Not in the least. Her heart was beating, loud and hard. Anticipation was an actual taste in her mouth—sharp and tart. "She's there, she's there. She has to be there…." She said it under her breath, a chant, an incantation, a prayer—as she slogged the ten feet from the porch to the woodshed.

She flipped the cracked leather latch. The plank door swung into the shadows beyond, creaking as it moved. The snow had piled up at the sill. Jilly stepped over it and down, onto the packed, cold dirt floor of the shed.

"It's in here? Something in here?" Will was right behind her, so close his warm breath stirred her tangled hair.

All at once, she was frightened. She didn't want to look. What would happen when she looked? Would reality turn sad and empty? Would her dream prove to be just that, nothing more than a transient projection of her hopeful heart?

Will clasped her shoulders with his strong hands. "Hey. You okay?"

It was enough. The sound of his voice, those fine, steady hands. She could manage it now. She could face looking into that box.

"I'm fine." She patted his left hand with her right. He let go. She stepped forward, toward the box in the corner at the edge of the stacks of waiting firewood. One step and then two.

And right then, as Jilly lifted her foot for that third step, Missy rose from the box, good ear first, followed quickly by her sweet little head and her furry kitty shoulders.

"I'll be damned," said Will, amazed.

Missy yawned hugely and lazily blinked her amber eyes at them, obviously just awakening from sleep.

Jilly was on her in two more steps. She reached down and scooped the cat up and buried her face in soft, warm calico fur. Instantly, Missy was purring, her body revving against Jilly's cheek. "Oh, Missy baby," she crooned into her cat's sweet tummy. "Merry Christmas, sweetheart. Merry, Merry Christmas." Overcome with gratitude, Jilly tipped her head back and sent a breathless prayer heavenward. "Thank you, Mavis. Thank you so much...."

Missy was squirming, reaching for Jilly's shoulder. Jilly let her climb up where she wanted to be.

"Thank you, *Mavis?*" Will asked from behind her.

Jilly whirled his way and opened her mouth to tell him everything. But before she let the words escape, she thought again.

The trouble was, he seemed such a practical man—except for his holiday phobia, which, while irrational, was certainly understandable, given all the awful things that had happened to him at Christmastime. If she told him that she was absolutely certain his dead grandmother had dropped in for a visit two nights in a row, she had a pretty clear picture of what would happen next.

He'd figure the bump on her head had scrambled her brain, after all. He'd whip out his cell and dial 911. And most likely, by now, the phone would be working again.

He'd have a helicopter full of EMTs and life-support equipment on its way here in five minutes flat.

And Jilly wasn't ready to go. Not yet. At the very least, she wanted her chance to rummage through the boxes in the back of that closet upstairs, a chance to see if the real Mavis had looked anything like the woman in her dreams.

She said, "It was just a little prayer, you know? A prayer of gratitude."

"To my grandmother?"

"Well, this was her place, after all. I kind of feel that she's here, watching over us. Don't you feel it, too?"

He was looking way too skeptical. "How did you know the cat was out here?"

She gave him a huge, bright smile. "Just feminine intuition, that's all. Just a feeling I had."

He wasn't buying. "For plain intuition, you were pretty damned excited to get out here and have a look."

"Intuition's like that sometimes. I have it and I'm just jumping up and down with enthusiasm over it."

He muttered something under his breath. She decided she'd probably be happier not knowing what. "We checked this whole shed, carefully, yesterday."

"And we missed her. Or she wasn't in here yet. I don't know, Will. I told you. It was just a feeling I had, that she'd be here this morning." She knew what he needed. Distracting. She cleared the distance between them and held out her purring cat. Missy purred all the louder and pawed the air, reaching for him. "Here. Hold Missy."

He jumped back so fast, he almost tripped on the snow-packed doorsill behind him. "Damn it, Jilly."

"Aw, now. What kind of attitude is that? You can do it. Come on. Now's your chance to make up for all that meanness yesterday."

"It's freezing out here," he grumbled, shoving his hands in the pockets of his slept-in jeans. "We should go back inside."

"First, you take Missy." She gave him her most serious look and schooled her voice to firmness. "Do it now."

And what do you know? He did. He yanked his hands from his pockets and held out his arms. Missy went to him eagerly, pawing for his shoulder, cuddling close, getting going with an outboard-motor-sized purr.

"Tell her you *like* her. Tell her you'll never reject her affection again."

Reluctantly, happier to see the damn cat than he ever would have admitted to the woman in the fluffy pajamas, the snow-filled boots and shearling coat who was now beaming happily up at him, Will petted the animal and made his apology. "Listen, Missy. It's great to see you. How about we let bygones be bygones?"

Jilly's wide smile got even wider. "Good job. Let's go inside."

"Oh, ye of little faith," Jilly teased when she found out that yesterday he'd left the cat supplies in the car.

Will was only too happy to trudge out there and get everything. While he was outside, they got power again, the old fridge revving to life and the overhead light in the kitchen popping on.

"Ta-da," Jilly sang out when he came through the

door, indicating the light above with a flourish. "Now you won't have to fool with the generator."

Once Missy was comfortable and digging into a nice, big bowl of cat food, they made some instant cappuccino and enjoyed their morning bowls of Froot Loops. Will had turned on the radio when they first came back inside, so they already knew that the storm had been a huge one. It was going to be a day or two—or even three—until a county snowplow could possibly get around to that long, winding driveway out there.

That fit in just fine with the plan that was beginning to take shape in Jilly's mind. She ate fast.

Will asked with an amused lift of a bronze eyebrow, "Going to a fire?"

"I want to get upstairs and check in that closet. Remember, you said you thought you could find a picture of your grandmother in there?"

He sipped from his mug. "What I want first is a bath and a shave. That okay with you?"

It wasn't. She was shamelessly impatient to see Mavis. But it wasn't her house and the treasures upstairs were not hers to investigate on her own. "Oh. Well, sure. No problem. I'll wait."

Her expression must have given her away. He suggested, "Look. Why don't you just go ahead and get after it? I think most of the pictures are in a couple of albums in a cardboard file box. You know the kind I mean?"

She nodded, and managed to restrain herself from licking her lips, she was so very eager.

"I'll be up to join you in a while. If you haven't figured out who Mavis is by then, I'll show you."

"Terrific."

"I still don't get why you're so jazzed over this."

"Uh, well, I've been staying in her house. And you've told me so much about her. I'm beginning to feel as if I know her. I want to put a face to my idea of her."

"Whatever." He shrugged and dipped up another big spoonful of cereal. She figured her explanation must have satisfied him, because he didn't ask her any more questions.

Will tried his phone again before he went to take his bath. Same as before. Nothing but static.

"Try yours."

She went upstairs, dug hers out of her purse and pressed Talk.

He was waiting for her at the foot of the stairs. "Well?"

"More static."

"I guess it's you and me and Missy, for now." He gave her the sweetest, most rueful grin.

"Merry Christmas, Will."

"Humph."

"What was that?"

"Do I *have* to say it?"

She just looked at him, patiently.

"Oh, what the hell. Merry Christmas, Jilly." He went in the bathroom and shut the door.

She headed back up the stairs. She was going to get

dressed and then she was going to get in that closet and check out those photo albums.

There were lots of boxes and a couple of trunks pushed back in the crawl space behind the closet, between the outside wall and the Sheetrock paneling. Jilly had the flashlight Will had left on the dresser last night, so it didn't take her long to find the file box. She dragged it out into the light. When she took off the dusty lid, she discovered two dog-eared photo albums, a baby book and more boxes full of loose pictures, mostly old, mostly black-and-white.

The baby book was Caitlin's. It had a teddy bear on the cover and the words *All About Baby* in faded pink letters. Inside were all of Caitlin's baby statistics, lovingly entered in a careful, round hand, from birth weight and length to favorite songs of the day—by the Andrews Sisters and Frank Sinatra. There was a lock of glossy black hair. Jilly smiled at that. Caitlin's hair was still glossy black, kept that way, no doubt, with a helping hand from Clairol. Her first word, "No," was noted, and the date of her first baby step. The pages for baby showers and friendly advice were blank, signs of the life they had led, a mother and daughter, up in the mountains, all on their own. There were a few photos glued onto the final pages: baby Caitlin in only a diaper, lying on her back on a bed, and Caitlin as a toddler, holding a toy shovel, standing in the clearing outside with the old house behind her, squinting into the sun.

The two photo albums, on quick examination, appeared to be roughly chronological. The first held very old pictures in sepia tones, carefully posed, of people Jilly didn't recognize. The men wore bowler hats and spats, the women high-necked white shirtwaists with mutton-chop sleeves. The second was page after page of yellowing black-and-whites. Jilly took note of the slim dark-haired girl who appeared about midway through that second album. She thought she could see the re-semblance to Caitlin and Will—and to the Mavis of her dreams.

But it was after she moved on to the boxes full of snapshots that she found what she was looking for, shots of an old woman out in the clearing, with three little boys who had to be Aaron, Will and Cade. A picture of that same woman sitting in the chair in the living area, knitting what looked like the afghan Jilly had slept be-neath just last night. And another of the woman and Caitlin, standing side-by-side on Main Street in New Venice, in front of the Highgrade. In that one, Caitlin was laughing, dark head thrown back. Whatever the joke was, the old woman seemed to be in on it. Her face was crinkled with humor, but she had her hand over her mouth, as if to keep the laughter in.

Jilly stared from one picture to the next. Her cheeks felt too warm and her heart was racing. She was looking at Mavis, she was certain of it. Because the old woman was the same woman she had seen in her dreams.

Chapter 10

Jilly's first reaction was elation. She felt lifted up, vindicated. Her dreams were verified as truth.

Close on the heels of excitement, a shiver of dread crawled beneath her skin. This really couldn't be happening. She hadn't *really* been visited by the spirit of Will's dead grandmother two nights running. Had she?

She heard Will's step on the rickety stairs. A frantic thrill raced through her, followed swiftly by the odd urge to toss everything back in the box and shove it into the closet, to pretend she hadn't been looking through it, hadn't found the face from her dreams.

But then again, what was to pretend? Will had no idea of the things she might have seen.

He came through the curtain and she turned, still holding that picture of Mavis and Caitlin on Main Street. "I think this must be your grandmother. Am I right?"

He crouched beside her and took the picture. He smelled so good and clean. His face was smooth, his hair still wet. "Yep. That's my grandma." He lightly touched the wrinkled face. "She always covered her mouth when she laughed. She had false teeth that never fit right. I think she might have been embarrassed about them."

Jilly was quiet, recalling the beautiful teeth of the Mavis in her dream. It was the first wrong note in this whole symphony of magical happenings. Maybe in the spirit world, you could have the things you'd never had in life, including a set of white, perfect teeth.

Or more than likely, the voice of reason whispered wisely, your dreams were just that: dreams.

It was all rationally explainable, really.

She'd wandered into Will's room sometime that first night, forgotten she'd been in there when that tree branch fell on her head, but incorporated the buried memory into her dream. At some point, she *had* seen a picture of Mavis. Someone at some time or another had mentioned to her that Will Bravo once had a dog named Snatch. After all, she and Will had grown up in the same small town. And now her two best friends had married his brothers. She probably subconsciously knew things about Will she had no clue of at the conscious level.

And Missy in the rag box? Just what she'd told Will: intuition. Nothing more.

Will was watching her. "What's going on?"

"Huh? Oh, nothing."

"You look sad."

Sad? Was she? Maybe a little. She'd grown rather enamored of the whole idea that her dreams might be visions, that Mavis McCormack had come to communicate with her from beyond the grave. It did make her just a tiny bit sad to admit that it all added up to nothing more than her subconscious playing a few cute tricks.

However, she could deal with feeling sad. She wasn't sure how she would deal with having to accept that what she'd seen in her dreams was real.

She smiled at Will. "Maybe I am sad. I've been thinking about your grandmother, wondering what her life was like. It seems that she must have been lonely. So many years living up here, all alone."

His brows drew together. "To me, she just seemed comfortable, at peace with herself and the world she lived in. I was only a kid, though. What did I know?"

He had on a charcoal-gray turtleneck sweater and he'd pushed the sleeves to his elbows. She laid her hand on his forearm. "I'll bet you did know. Better than just about anybody else."

He looked down at her hand and then up into her eyes.

And everything changed. All at once, she was acutely aware of the silky hairs on his arm, the warmth of his flesh, of hard muscle beneath taut skin. She watched his Adam's apple move up and down as he swallowed—and found she was swallowing right along with him.

She dragged her gaze downward and let go of his arm, fast. "Come on," she said briskly, grabbing the scattered photos, dropping them into the open box. "Help me put these away. We have so much to do and only so many hours to do it in."

"Jilly."

She made herself look at him. And there it was again, that burning awareness, that lovely blooming feeling in her stomach, the sense of connection, of being pulled into him, the certainty that something absolutely wonderful was about to happen very soon....

Not.

They'd been over that. He didn't want to get anything started, and that was fine with her.

He was the one who looked away that time. When he looked back, the dangerous moment had passed. He asked, suspiciously, "What, exactly, do we have to do?"

She felt relief—honestly, she did—that they hadn't done anything foolish, like fall into each other's arms and start kissing madly. She had an agenda and making passionate, all-consuming love with Will would only distract her from what needed doing.

Her plan had been formulating since last night, when he'd gotten honest with her and told her all the reasons he had for hating Christmas. It was a good plan, and she wasn't giving up on it just because she'd realized that his dead grandma hadn't been dropping in on her at night, after all. Okay, her subconscious had been playing tricks on her. And why, she asked herself, would her subconscious do that?

Well, because it was trying to tell her something.

What had Will said to her, that first night, in her dream? *Help me, Jilly. Help me out. God, do I need it....*

It all fit together just perfectly and there was nothing supernatural about it. She had sensed a truth about Will and that truth had spoken to her through her dream.

He needed her help. And she was going to give it to

him. By the time the county snowplow got around to clearing the long driveway out front, Will Bravo would be Christmas-friendly. Jillian Diamond would see to that.

"Jilly," he said, when they were back in the kitchen, and she had started assembling the ingredients for dried apple, sausage and toasted pecan stuffing. "Do we have to do this?"

"We do." She opened the fridge and got out the sausage. "You're going to love it. I need a frying pan."

He opened the cabinet in the side of the stove and pulled out a lovely well-seasoned cast-iron one. "You know we'd both just as soon have something simple, something straight out of a nice, big can."

She put the pan on the stove, grabbed a match and lit the burner. "There are times when we are called upon to go all out. Times that demand we sit down to a true feast."

"Times like Christmas," he said glumly.

She blew out the match. "Like Christmas, exactly. Pass me that sausage." He handed it over. She peeled back the label and rolled the meat free of the white butcher paper and into the pan. She held out her hand. "Wooden spoon?"

He turned to the earthenware jar with all the utensils standing up in it, grabbed what she'd asked for and slapped it into her palm. The meat started sizzling.

She adjusted the flame and began breaking up the sausage with the spoon. "Get out the turkey, will you? Rinse it inside and out and wipe it dry with paper towels.

Oh, and don't forget to remove the giblets. They're probably in the neck cavity. Wash them, too."

He grunted unwillingly, but he did turn and pull the bird from the fridge.

"I want to get the turkey in the oven," she said. "Then we'll be free to go out and find ourselves a tree."

"My first choice would have to be a silver-tip fir," Jilly announced. "I like the tiered effect of the branches, combined with the lush thickness of the needles. And that silvery-green color. Oh, I do love that." She shivered, mostly from pleasure but partly because it was cold outside. They stood knee-deep in snow at the back of the house, all rigged out in their coats and boots, wool hats and thick gloves. Will had an axe he'd taken from the shed.

"We don't have a permit," he warned, his breath coming out as a white vapor in the icy air. "We can't just wander out in the woods and chop down any tree that catches our eye. We're surrounded by national forest, in case you didn't notice."

"Oh, stop grumbling."

He hefted the axe. "I'm not grumbling. I'm making a valid point."

Jilly brought up a hand to shield her eyes against the blinding glare of bright sun on new snow. The trees started fifty or sixty feet from the kitchen windows. The land there sloped sharply upward into what appeared to be a mountain. In any case, it was a large hill, covered in evergreens, and it went on for a long way, up toward the ice-blue winter sky. "How big is this property?"

"Why?"

She sent him a chiding look. "Work with me here."

"Ten acres." He pointed toward the hill. "And as you can see, at least half the acreage is on a serious slant. Where we have trees, they're pretty thick. They tend to grow with bare spots and uneven branches, not what you want in a Christmas tree."

Jilly rubbed her gloves together. "Well, then. I guess we'd better start looking."

"Why did I know you were going to say that?"

Right then, Jilly thought she saw movement—in the trees at the base of the hill. "Do you see that?"

He squinted toward where she pointed. "I see trees. A lot of trees."

"No. Something moving. An animal, I think."

"I don't see anything now. Probably a deer."

"No, it was smaller than a deer."

"Jilly, around here, we've got deer and raccoons and brown bears and mountain lions. And that's just for starters."

"It's gone now, whatever it was." Jilly shivered—and not from cold. "I hope it wasn't a lion. They scare me. You never know what they'll do."

"You want to forget the tree?" he suggested hopefully. "I could go get my hunting rifle and we could track the unknown animal instead."

"Not a chance."

It took about a half an hour. By then, Jilly was cold enough to compromise a little. The tree they found was in the woods on the side of the house where they'd trooped around calling for Missy the day before. It was a Douglas fir, about six and a half feet tall and a little sparse on one side.

"But we'll put it by your chair, in front of the window in the living area," she said, "with the bad side turned so we can't see it."

"You're saying I should start chopping, right?"

"Yes. The quicker we get it cut down and put up in the house, the quicker we can start figuring out what to do for decorations."

His expression turned especially bleak. "We're going to decorate it."

"Oh, come on. It's a Christmas tree, remember? You put it up in the house and then you *decorate* it. Now, just cut it down, will you? It's cold out here."

"Okay, stand over there."

"Because?"

"Can't you ever in your life just follow instructions?"

"You know, I could ask you the same question."

"Jilly. If you stand over there, you won't get hit by flying wood chips and the damn thing's unlikely to fall on you."

"Well, all right. That makes sense." She trotted over to where he'd pointed. He raised the axe. But before he struck the first blow, he lowered it and turned to her.

"Oh, Will," she moaned. "What now?"

"In a couple of days, we'll be able to get out of here. You're not just going to drive off and leave me with this thing in the living room, are you?"

"What are you after?"

"A commitment to tree removal. From you."

"Since we'll be making the decorations, everything should be disposable. Taking it down won't be a big deal."

"We're *making* decorations?"

"You have a better suggestion?"

"Let's get back to my original request. Are you going to help me take this damn thing down?"

"Okay, no problem. I'll help you take it down before I go."

"Thank you very much."

"Start chopping."

Under ordinary circumstances, Jilly would have put the tree in water with tree preserver to keep it green. But they were improvising here, with the equipment on hand. No tree stand presented itself, and they'd be taking it down in a day or two anyway. So Will nailed on a wooden stand of two-by-four scraps he found in the shed. They carried it inside and stood it up in front of the window next to the easy chair.

Jilly stepped back and drew in a big breath through her nose. "Oh, smell that. I love the smell of evergreen, don't you? And it looks great. You can't even see the uneven part." Will's radio was still playing, softly, in the kitchen, still tuned to NPR, which was cooperating nicely now, with a program of Christmas tunes in honor of the day. One of her favorites was on right then, "Holly, Jolly Christmas," a real classic, sung by Burl Ives. She turned to Will.

He was watching her. And he was almost smiling. Was that admiration she saw in those beautiful deep-blue eyes? She got those lovely flutters in her stomach again. Her cheeks felt warm, her heart beat faster. She was maybe four steps away from him. She wanted to close that small distance.

She could see it, just how it would be.

He would hold out those strong arms to her and she would move into them. He would wrap her close in his warm and cherishing embrace. She would offer her mouth. He would claim it.

Oh, yes. A long, sweet Christmas kiss. In front of the tree they'd just cut fresh, themselves.

"Does your enthusiasm ever flag?" His voice was rough—and soft at the same time, one notch above a whisper. He wasn't smiling anymore. He was looking at her mouth.

What was she *thinking?* She shook herself. Firmly. "Don't tell a soul, but now and then, I can get a little down."

"Like yesterday?"

She glanced at the old sofa bed. Missy was curled there, asleep on one of the thin throw pillows. Safe. "It hit me hard, her disappearing. Mostly because I knew it was all my fault."

He started to argue. "It wasn't your—"

"Will."

"What?"

"We've already been through that. Let's not start on it again."

After a moment, he nodded. "Good idea. So. Decorations are next, right?"

"Good gravy, you should see yourself. For the first time, you mentioned decorations without scowling."

"You'll have me singing 'Jingle Bells' before we're through."

That brought on a clear visual of a teenaged Will opening a closet door and finding Monty and Mitzi in flagrante delicto. He was remembering the same thing. His devilish smile told her so.

"Well, it's Christmas," she said. "Anything's possible, right?"

"So you keep telling me."

They were doing it again, staring at each other. She had that dizzying, falling feeling as if she were drowning deliciously, right there in his eyes.

Speak, she thought. Say something *now.* "I did come prepared for tree decorating."

"You were going to cut down a tree all by yourself?"

"You don't think I could have managed it?"

"I'm sure you can do anything you put your mind to."

She gave him a slow smile. "That's what I like to hear. And I brought construction paper and scissors, glue and glitter. It's upstairs in my suitcase. I'll just—"

"I've got a better idea."

The way he said that sent a lovely, warm shiver quivering all through her.

He said, "Upstairs, in that closet where you found the pictures, you'll also find a couple of big boxes of Christmas stuff."

The lights were the old-fashioned kind, heavy black wires with big multicolored bulbs. There was rumpled gold garland and a variety of dime-store glass ornaments, most of them faded with age.

"This stuff is a little the worse for wear," Will said when they opened the dusty boxes and had a look inside.

"I love it. All of it. Every last inch of ragged garland, every ancient ornament."

He looked hopeful. "That means no craft projects, right?"

"Let's haul it all downstairs."

By one in the afternoon, they had the lights, the garland and every last faded ornament hanging on their tree. They took a break to share a can of Campbell's tomato soup. They wanted to eat light, because dinner was going to be a feast and it was only a few hours away. Over the soup, she convinced him to turn up the radio a little so she could hear her Christmas favorites while they cooked.

As the savory smell of cider-glazed roasting turkey mingled with the piney scent of the tree, they got to work on the big meal. There was to be pumpkin soup with sage and crème fraîche for starters. With the bird, they'd have gingered cranberry sauce, roasted root vegetables, the stuffing, corn strips with chives and cheddar, green beans with sherry vinegar and soft wheat rolls. She'd planned for two desserts: apple tart with tangy cranberry swirl topping and chocolate pecan pie.

Will was an angel. A miracle. A total surprise. He chopped and sliced and diced and shredded, whatever she asked of him, he did. He found a yellowed linen tablecloth in the bedroom bureau and he spread it on the table. He polished up the mismatched flatware, brought a couple of pewter candle holders down from a top shelf and stood two white household emergency candles in them.

At a little before five, they were ready to eat. Will carved the turkey. He did a fine job. Then he poured the wine—they made do with a pair of juice tumblers for wineglasses.

Jilly lit the candles and they sat down. They raised their juice glasses and toasted each other, the season—and Mavis, for the use of her fine house. Then they ate. For a very long time.

When they were both sure they couldn't eat another bite, they cleared off the table and put away everything but the tempting desserts that still waited untouched on the counter. They played Scrabble for a couple of hours.

Jilly won.

Will was sure she had cheated. "Do you know how many times I've played this game?" He answered his own question. "Hundreds. Thousands. Nobody takes me at Scrabble."

"Oh, stop beating your chest or I won't let you have any chocolate pecan pie."

"Just admit it. You cheated."

"I do not cheat at board games. I'm above such things."

"When I went to the bathroom, you—"

"No. I didn't. Wrong, wrong, wrong."

"But...*zestfully,* on a triple-word score, the Z on a double? I don't think so."

"I beat you fair and square. Live with it. And come on, let's get some water boiling so we can have a little instant cappuccino with our pie and apple-cranberry tart."

He tried to keep scowling, but he was having too much fun. "All right. I concede victory to you."

"There's nothing quite so admirable as a graceful loser."

"Do me a big favor. Don't rub it in."

They put the game away and served themselves dessert. Then they turned off all the lights except the ones on the tree and they sat together on the old sofa bed, sipping instant cappuccino, eating apple tart and pecan pie.

"The tree is beautiful," she said. The old-fashioned lights reflected off the faded bulbs. Those bulbs gleamed and twinkled just as brightly as they must have when they were new.

"God. This pecan pie…"

"Will. You're groaning."

"I can't help myself. I'm amazed and humbled. You beat me at Scrabble. You appreciate franks and beans. You love mac and cheese. But when you set your mind to it, damn it, can you cook."

"Amazed and humbled. I really like the sound of that."

"But maybe I'm just relieved."

"I like amazed and humbled better. But I'm interested. Why are you relieved?"

"You didn't insist on a gift exchange. I think I hate that part the most. It's so over the top anymore. Stores start pushing you to buy, buy, buy before Halloween."

"I really wanted to do gifts."

"And here I thought you'd risen above the crass and commercial aspects of the holiday."

"No way. I'm as crass and commercial as they come."

"So what stopped you?"

"I just couldn't think of what to give you on such short notice. And then there was the little problem of the limited shopping opportunities up here on your grandmother's ten acres. I did consider making them. I could have gotten us into the craft project you managed to avoid when you came up with the boxes of decorations—origami, maybe. Or macramé."

"Some things you shouldn't do to a man."

"So true. I was afraid if I tried it, you might become violent."

"So you're saying, you ordinarily do all that? You go all out with the gifts?"

"That's right. I shopped and wrapped for everyone before I left Sacramento. Bought for my folks and my sisters and all their little darlings, for Janey and Cade and Ceil and Aaron."

"You send cards?"

"I do. Over a hundred now and the list is always growing."

He was shaking his head. "Sorry. I don't get it. It's too much work, and for what, really? People get crazy during the holidays, you know damn well they do. Expectations get too high. The suicide rate soars."

"Oh, relax. Nobody's making you do anything you don't want to do. All I'm trying to get across to you is you don't have to hide out here until the season is past. You could come down from the mountain, you know?

Join your family for Christmas dinner. Expect a miracle, instead of disaster."

"If you're cooking, I might come."

"You are being altogether too appreciative." She took his empty plate and mug from him, set it, with hers, on the table at the head of the sofa bed. "I keep waiting for you to get mean again."

"I won't. On that level anyway, I'm a changed man. I've accepted the fact that I really do like you. And your damn cat, too."

"And next year? Will you be holed up here all over again?"

He faked a frown. "What do you want from me?"

What she wanted, she was trying very hard to keep remembering, she wasn't going to get. But he did look fabulous by tree-light. And here they were, all alone, with all this time on their hands, getting along so well, enjoying each other in *almost* every sense of the word.

And he was single and she was single and they were both adults and sometimes the best way to get rid of a big appetite was to simply go ahead and eat. Indulge yourself. Worry about paying the price later—if there was even going to be any price.

Certainly, it had to be possible for two reasonably mature adults to have a lovely, romantic, sensual interlude and remain on good terms when it was over. Who could say? Maybe it wouldn't have to end. Maybe they'd discover they were meant for each other. Like Jane and Cade—and Aaron and Celia.

Stranger things had happened.

Okay, okay. She could see the writing on the steamy

window. Will Bravo was *not* going to suddenly realize she was the woman for him. He'd already found the woman for him. And she had died. He hadn't really gotten over her, and he wasn't looking for anyone to take her place.

And that was fine. Jilly wasn't looking for anything permanent either. Necessarily.

Jilly sighed. "What was the question?"

He had leaned in closer. He was looking at her mouth again. "I really want to kiss you."

She was looking at his mouth, too. Such a fine and tempting mouth it was. "I can't believe you said that."

"It would be a mistake, huh?"

"Probably." Her voice came out sounding so husky. She was thinking, *Probably, but do I care?*

And the answer? Less and less as each second ticked by.

"We could call it my Christmas present." He was whispering now. No need to speak louder. His mouth was just inches from hers, his breath warm on her lips, smelling of apples and chocolate and coffee.

"You want a kiss from me for Christmas?"

"I do. I want it a lot."

"And we *are* trying to build you some positive Christmas memories, now aren't we?"

"It's in a good cause."

"Oh, yes. I think so."

He lifted a hand and oh-so-tenderly smoothed her hair, following the line of it along the side of her face and under, until his palm lay curved, warm and encompassing, against the back of her neck. He pulled her toward him, that crucial last inch or so.

And at last, she felt his lips touch hers.

Chapter 11

It wasn't like her dream. He didn't burn her lips off.

He melted them.

Jilly sighed in pure pleasure, parting her lips slightly, just enough to tempt him to slip his tongue inside. He did.

Oh, yes. Oh, yes, yes, yes...

She slid her tongue along the bottom of his. He moaned. She liked that. She moaned right back and reached up a hand, clasping that hard, muscled shoulder of his, then caressing her way up, over the soft wool of that charcoal-gray sweater until she could slip her fingers into the silky hair at his nape.

He moaned again. And he guided her down against the skinny little pillows at the head of the sofa bed. He kissed her mouth for a long time and she kissed him right back, their tongues sparring and sliding, occasionally pausing to share a smile, mouth-to-mouth, and then delving in again.

Oh, it was lovely.

When he finally opened those deep-blue eyes and looked down at her, she found herself thinking how really great it was to be alive. You never knew what might happen. Someone mean and awful could decide to make a little effort to be a decent human being and then, before you knew it, you might find yourself discovering he was the best kisser you'd ever met.

"Merry Christmas, Will."

"Merry Christmas, Jilly. Thank you for my present."

"My pleasure." And it had been. Her pleasure in the extreme.

"I'd like to do a lot more than kiss you."

"I kind of picked that up. But you're conflicted, right? I mean, my best friends, your brothers, all that. Not to mention your mother."

He gave her a crooked smile. "See what you're doing to me? For a minute there, I actually forgot all about her and the trouble she can make."

She reached up and ran a finger along the fine, manly line of his nose. It was so nice. To touch him. To have him looking at her the way he'd been looking at her for most of the day. With admiration. With kindling desire. She was sorely tempted to explore this situation further, to get into it in delicious detail.

And anyway, why keep denying it? They were past the denial stage. He wanted her. She wanted him. Oh, yes. She did. She really, really wanted him.

But then again, she was like that. When Jilly really wanted something, good sense flew right out the window. It shamed her to admit it now, but she had really wanted Benny Simmerson. And look where that had gotten her.

"I hate to be the voice of reason," she whispered. "It's so totally *not* me."

He looked gorgeously rueful. "You think we'd better sleep on it, don't you?"

"Yeah. I do. I think we'd better sleep on it *alone*."

Jilly had just climbed between the cool sheets of the bed upstairs when her phone started ringing. The bleating sound took her totally off-guard. After all, it hadn't rung for over two days now.

She grabbed it off the night table.

"Merry Christmas, darlin' girl." Caitlin's voice was husky and low and way too sexy for a woman who would be a grandma any day now. "We ought to put in a land line up there. I tried to call yesterday. And twice earlier today. I couldn't get through."

"No kidding. I guess you tried Will's phone, too?"

"He doesn't much like to hear from me this time of year. He doesn't much like to hear from anybody. But I guess you've figured that out by now."

"Well, Caitlin. I can't say about the phones. I'd imagine the storm knocked them out."

There was a tiny pause, then Caitlin asked sweetly, "Jilly honey, you mad at me?"

"Now, why would I be mad at you?"

"Oh, come on. You're mad. You are. But look at it this way, I never lied to you, now did I?"

"Yes, you did."

"You didn't ask. I didn't tell. That's not a lie."

"Have you ever considered running for public office?"

"With my past? Are you crazy?"

"Caitlin, I'd really like to know, was Celia in on this with you?"

"She was not. You know Celia. Not a tricky bone in her whole body. It was just one of those things."

"Just one of *what* things?"

"Things that happen. Things where everything works out all by itself. You needed a house in the mountains and you called Celia. She thought of my ma's house and said you ought to call me about it."

"And when I did call you, you lied."

"Sweetie. Face it. If I'd told you he was up there, would you be there now?"

"Of course not."

"Well, okay then. What else is there to say?"

"A lot. You've got to start reining yourself in a little, Caitlin, you've got to stop treating people as if they're pawns in some big chess game you're playing."

"Havin' a good time?"

"Well, I wasn't at first."

"But you are now, right?"

"Caitlin, I know that whatever I say to you is likely to come back to haunt me at a later date. So I think I'll just keep my mouth shut."

"Now, Jilly. Is that any way to be?"

"Are you at Jane's?"

"I got back to the Highgrade about twenty minutes

ago. My newest daughter-in-law can cook. What a meal. I won't have to eat for a week, at least. Why?"

"Maybe I'd like to say Merry Christmas to my friends. Maybe I'm concerned that they've been worried about me. For all they know I've been stuck alone in an old house way up in the mountains in a blizzard, with the phones on the blink. Maybe they'd like to hear that I'm all right."

"Well, yeah, they were a little worried. But they put their heads together and figured out pretty quick that you weren't alone up there. And then, over dinner tonight, they got on me until I confessed that I sent you to Ma's house without mentioning that Will was going to be there, too."

Missy jumped up on the end of the bed. She was looking only slightly sulky to be locked away from Will for another whole night.

"Jilly, you still there?"

"Barely."

"I thought for a minute you'd hung up on me."

"I have to admit, I'm tempted. So you told my friends how you tricked me."

"*Tricked* you? I never used that word."

"I'd better call them."

"Whatever you think."

"Maybe *you* ought to call Will."

"And have him shout at me on Christmas? I'll pass."

Jilly thought of the kiss they'd shared not too long before and smiled to herself. If Caitlin did call him, she might be surprised at how well he was taking being snowed in with the woman he had claimed to despise.

Not that Jilly would even hint at such a thing. It would only encourage Caitlin to keep on with her meddling.

Caitlin was still talking. "In years to come, you'll thank me. And look at it this way, all I did was give you an opportunity. And then along comes that big storm. Now, nobody could call that my fault. So in the end, what you two do with bein' stuck there together is completely up to you."

"You played me, Caitlin. You know that you did. All that stuff about how *primitive* it was going to be, on my own here in this isolated house, all the tips on how to start the stove, how to work the generator in case the power went out."

Caitlin laughed that husky, pure-sex laugh of hers. "Had you goin' there, didn't I?"

"Did anyone ever tell you that you are absolutely shameless?"

Caitlin sighed. "Well, sure. All the time."

"I have to go. I need to call my friends and let them know I'm all right."

"Jilly?"

"What now?"

"If you run into my ma's ghost, you be sure to tell her hi for me."

Jilly could hear the laughter in Caitlin's voice, but a cold shiver skittered up her spine anyway. "Very funny. Good night." She hung up before Caitlin could say another word and immediately dialed Jane.

Her friend answered on the second ring. "Jilly. Thank God you're okay."

"I'm fine. It's been…an adventure. The phones have been out."

"I know. I called and called."

"Well, they're working now. I didn't even realize they were back on until I got a call from Caitlin and—"

Jane cut her off. "Hold on, okay?" She spoke to someone on her end. Jilly recognized the other voice. Jane came back on the line, "Now, where were we?"

"Is that Celia?"

"It is. She and Aaron are staying the night. She wants to talk to you."

"You sound so serious. Honestly, I'm perfectly safe."

"We're just so relieved to hear from you—and you'd better call your mother. She's about to send out a posse."

"I will, I will."

"You said Caitlin called you…."

"That's right, a few minutes ago."

"We had it out with her at dinner tonight. We told her she had to stop manipulating people. You know how I adore her, but sometimes I think she needs a good spanking. Ceil's mortified, since she was the one who suggested you call Caitlin in the first place. She's sure you're going to think—"

"Put her on."

"I will. Jilly?"

"What?"

"You're *sure* you're all right?"

"Oh, Janey. You know me. Nothing gets me down for long."

"And Will?"

"He's fine, too."

"You're getting along?"

"Yes. I'll tell you all about it later. Maybe."

Jane laughed. "Miss you. Wish you were here."

"Merry Christmas."

Celia came on the line apologizing. "Jilly, I swear to you. I didn't know that Will would be up there. I assumed he'd be here, with the family, for Christmas. Turns out Janey knew, but I didn't get the story from her until after you'd left Sacramento."

"How did Jane know?"

"When she asked Cade to invite Will for Christmas dinner, Cade told her why there was no way Will would come, about he goes up to Mavis's old house every year now, since Nora died—and wait a minute. Do you even know about what happened to Nora? Am I making any sense at all?"

"You're making perfect sense. I do know about Nora. Will told me. And I don't blame you for a thing, so get that thought out of your mind."

"Oh, good. I'm so relieved."

"How are you? How's the baby?"

"Oh, pu-lease. You saw me two weeks ago. The words *elephantine* and *enormous* should come to mind."

"You look great."

"Right. Jilly, I am so sorry about all this."

"Don't be. Truthfully, everything's worked out fine. Will and I are getting along great. We've…made the most of an uncomfortable situation."

"But he wanted to be alone and so did you." Jilly heard Jane's voice in the background. Then Celia said, "Jane wants to know where you'll go when the roads are cleared. She says you should come here, stay with her and Cade for a few days."

Jilly hadn't a clue right then what she would do when the roads were passable. Originally, she'd intended to stay at the old house until the second of January. And then, when she found Will here, she'd wanted to get out as soon as she possibly could.

But now?

She thought of his kiss again, felt her midsection melting. At this point, it was anybody's guess what would happen once she was free to go elsewhere. She had no appointments scheduled for another whole week. And her columns were no problem. She turned them in via e-mail, anyway.

"Tell Jane I'll give her a call."

"I will. And Jilly?"

"Yeah?"

"Merry Christmas."

"Merry Christmas to you, Ceil. Get your rest. Take your vitamins."

Jilly's sisters were in Reno with their families, at her mother's for the night. She called them all there. After she'd reassured them she was fine, she listened to a chorus of thank-yous for the gifts she'd sent.

Once she said goodbye to her family, she checked her e-mail. Incredible, the amount of mail that could pile up with just two days of down time. A lot of it was junk mail, links to her favorite on-line shopping sites where after-Christmas sales were already in progress. She grinned to herself. She ought to buy something—

just so she could tell Will that she'd been to the after-Christmas sales and she hadn't had to jump over a single dying man to do it.

She went to sleep around eleven. If she dreamed of a certain man's exquisite kisses, that was her business. But in the morning, when she woke, she had no memory of any visits from Mavis.

Jilly raised her mug of instant cappuccino high. "Happy birthday, Will."

He grinned at her, a shy grin that tugged at her heart-strings, reminding her of the boy he must have been once, the boy whose birthday was too often forgotten. "You remembered."

They shared a long look. Jilly felt warm all over. Will had already been outside and come in to report he'd seen no sign of the snowplow. On the radio, all the talk centered on what had happened during the recent storms. "The worst in two decades," one announcer kept declaring. There were tales of people trapped in their cars, people stranded, digging snow caves, somehow surviving in spite of the terrible cold. And now it was over, not even the experts could say for sure how long it was going to take the Tahoe area to dig out from under.

Jilly figured they'd be stuck here at least till tomorrow. Possibly till Friday.

The thought sent her pulse pounding. Another day, at least, alone with Will, another day where she didn't have to make an actual choice to be here. Right now, the only decision before them was how intimate they would be while they remained snowbound in this house together.

"My phone's working," she told him. "I got a call last night."

He knew instantly. "Caitlin."

"I told her she ought to call you—but don't worry. She said she wasn't up to listening to you shout at her on Christmas."

There was a pause. It was a lovely one—but then, lately, all the pauses were lovely ones. They sipped from their mugs and they looked at each other and the morning sun shone through the window, bringing out the gold lights in his brown hair.

Finally, Will said softly, "I wouldn't have shouted at her."

"I know. But I didn't tell her that."

"Good thinking. If she knew how much I'm enjoying your company, I'd never hear the end of it."

"Your secret is safe with me."

"I didn't say it was a secret. I just said I'm not in the mood to discuss it with Caitlin."

Was that good news? Oh, she didn't know. She didn't care. She was feeling just a tiny bit addled, a little goofy, a tad confused. And very, very excited.

"After I talked to Caitlin, I called Jane. We wished each other a merry Christmas. I talked to Celia, too. She and Aaron were staying there for the night."

She waited for him to respond to that, thinking maybe he'd remark on how everyone would razz them now, about being snowed in here together for days and days. But he didn't say anything. He just looked at her, a slight smile curving his mouth. As if he liked looking at her, as if he liked it very, very much. As if he'd like to look at her with all of her clothes off.

As if he planned to do just that, very soon.

She set down her mug. "You should have a birthday cake. I'm pretty sure I can fake it with the ingredients on hand."

Now he was looking at her mouth. He seemed to really like that—to look at her mouth. He certainly did it enough.

He said, tenderly, "We've already got desserts running out our ears."

That warm, melting feeling was spreading—out from her stomach, down low in her belly, along her legs, up through her chest and down her arms. "Admit it," she said. "You'd like a cake."

"Well. Maybe a small one...."

"With a candle in it."

"Jilly, you think of everything."

"I try."

Right then, she was thinking that there was absolutely no way they would make it through the next night in separate beds, and she was wondering if she would live to regret what she was thinking.

Then again, maybe she was just thinking too much.

After they cleaned up the breakfast, Will said he wanted to put in a little effort at digging out the driveway. "There's no telling when the plow will get around to us. Might as well get a start on it."

Action. Yes. Fresh air and exercise. Ordinarily, Jilly wasn't all that big on physical fitness, but today, well, she had an excess of energy and clearing the driveway seemed as good a way as any to work some of it off. "You have two shovels?"

"There's no need for you to—"

"I want to. And I've certainly got the time. It's not going to take me all day to bake you a cake."

So they piled on their outerwear and got the shovels from the shed and spent the morning shoveling—well, to be strictly truthful, Will spent the morning shoveling. Jilly shoveled, too, but she took a break now and then—a bathroom break, a cup-of-cappuccino break, a stand-in-front-of-the-heater-until-the-shivering-stops break.

Even with breaks, it was hard work. And Jilly thought she saw that animal again—it was a flash of brown and white, sliding through the trees at the edge of the clearing. She stopped shoveling to watch for another sight of it, and Will teased her that she was daydreaming on the job. She shrugged and went back to work.

When they put the shovels away at noon, she was sore and sweating beneath her heavy coat. And for all the work they'd done, there was still a lot of driveway buried in three feet of snow.

"Every little bit helps," Will said. "Tomorrow, we'll get farther. And maybe the plow will show up."

Jilly's shoulders and arms were aching. "Tomorrow, I may not be able to move. What I want right now is a long, hot bath."

"The bathroom is at your disposal."

When they got inside, she made him go first. She knew he'd be quick and then she could relax in there, take her time, lolling and lingering. There were few things Jilly enjoyed quite so much as a long soak in a scented tub. And today, after doing all that shoveling, she really needed it.

But somehow, once she took off her clothes and climbed into the lovely fragrant water, she couldn't relax, couldn't tune out the fact that Will was on the other side of the bathroom door and as soon as she got done in there, she could be with him.

"That was fast." Will pulled the platter of sliced turkey from the fridge. "Want a sandwich?"

"I would love one."

He sent her what he clearly intended as a quick, affectionate glance. But then he must have seen it, right there in her eyes—what she really wanted, and how powerfully she wanted it. He turned to her fully and held out his hand.

She needed no further urging. She ran to him.

Chapter 12

Will gathered her into his arms.

Was there ever a woman who smelled this good? He buried his face in her fragrant hair and breathed deep. She nuzzled his shoulder. He kissed the crown of her head, loving the feel of the silky strands against his lips.

"You want this, right?" He cradled her face in both hands and made her look at him. "You've made up your mind. Is that the message I'm getting here?"

She pressed those sweet lips together and nodded.

He couldn't help smiling at her expression. "Scared?"

She stuck out that obstinate chin. "Are you kidding? Me?" Then she sighed. "Well, all right. Maybe a little." She held up her thumb and forefinger, with a quarter inch of space between them. "This much. No more."

"If you want to back out—"

"Uh-uh. I'm up for this."

"You're sure?"

She giggled up at him. "Are you trying to talk me out of it, now?"

"No way."

It was probably foolish and they'd both live to regret it, but hell. She was willing. And he ached to have her. And maybe, in the end, there were just some things even a man who wasn't in the market for a woman couldn't turn down.

But there was a problem. One that had only occurred to him when he saw she'd decided to carry this thing between them to its natural conclusion.

He'd brought no contraceptives. He never did, not to his grandmother's house. He always came up here on his own and no one ever dropped in for a visit. Opportunities for sexual encounters were nil. Or they had been.

Until Jilly.

And that had been fine with him—until Jilly.

He touched the bump on her forehead. "This is looking pretty good."

"You have an inordinate interest in the bump on my head."

"I'm just glad, every time I look at it, that it isn't any worse."

"It looks like hell, and you know it. But the good news is, I think I'll still be able to lead a full and productive life."

"It would appear so."

"And you're stalling."

"Maybe."

She kissed his chin. "Why?"

"Because right now, under any other circumstances,

I'd be begging you to hold it right there while I ran down to the corner drug store."

The light dawned in those gray-blue eyes. "Better safe than sorry, you mean?"

"That's right." Now he couldn't read her expression. "What, exactly, are you thinking?"

"Well, it's like this," she said, and then wrinkled her nose at him in lieu of finishing her sentence.

"Jilly. Spill it."

"Okay, okay. I've got them."

He blinked. "Condoms? You've got—"

"Yes." She tipped her head back and let out a groan. "Oh, I just know what you're thinking. That I came up here to hook up with you, after all, that your original suspicions about me were true."

"That's not what I'm thinking."

"Right."

"Jillian. I swear to you I'm thinking nothing of the kind. And anyway, at this point, I don't give a damn why you came up here. In fact, if you *had* come up here because you just couldn't wait any longer to make mad, passionate love with me, you wouldn't hear me complaining. The only thing you'd hear from me would be, 'Hey, let me help you with that.'"

She turned her head to the side and slid him a look. "Really? You're past caring why I came up here?"

"Past it? It's so far behind me, I don't even remember anymore that I ever did care."

"And you're not thinking that I planned to seduce you?"

He cupped her face again, and lowered his mouth to

brush a kiss against those sweet, sweet lips. "No, I'm not. But please. Don't let that stop you from going ahead and seducing me anyway."

She smiled against his mouth—and then pulled back enough to announce, "It's a matter of principle."

"I understand completely."

"Oh, you do not."

"Yes, I do." She started to argue further. He put a finger against her lips. "Wait. Listen." He tried to remember, to get the wording exact. "'Our bodies—and our health and well-being—are our own responsibility. Too many women aren't prepared when the moment comes. Or they tell themselves they plan to say no—and then find themselves changing their minds, saying yes. The point? Say no. Say yes. As a grown-up self-sufficient woman, it's your choice. But no matter what you plan to say, be ready to be safe.'"

Her cheeks were adorably flushed. "Will Bravo. You've been reading my column."

"I remembered that one in particular. I thought it was right on the money."

"But you...I mean, you, I..."

He grinned down at her. "Jillian Diamond at a loss for words. This has to be a first."

She made a face at him. "Treasure the moment."

"I am—and I'll admit, you were never supposed to know. No one was ever supposed to know. It was my guilty secret that 'Ask Jillian' had become every bit as much a part of my morning routine as Froot Loops and Belgian Crème cappuccino. That's why I made such an effort the other night, asking you those questions about what you put in your column."

"You were hoping I'd never guess that you already knew?"

"You got it."

"You don't seem especially guilty about it now."

"All that's behind me. Somewhere between when you blew in the door Sunday and that kiss last night, I've given up trying to resist you."

She sighed. He felt her soft, small breasts rise and fall against his chest. Her eyes were gleaming. She slid her hands up over his shoulders and her fingers brushed the back of his neck, threading up into his hair. "You're surrendering totally?"

"Yeah. I'm gone. There's no turning back. I think it's only fair that you kiss me now."

She obliged, lifting that incredible mouth and parting her lips beneath his.

He loved the way she tasted. It was every bit as good as how she smelled. He slipped his tongue inside, swept it around in that wonderful wet, slick heat. He could kiss her forever. That would be fine with him. They could stand there, in the kitchen, with the warm steam from her bath all around them, kissing until the rest of the day went by and the night came, and then just kissing some more.

It would be better, though, if they were both naked. And then, eventually, he was going to have to do something about how powerfully he wanted her—so much that it hurt.

But in a good way.

She'd come out of the bathroom in a red fleecy sweater that ended just above her waist. She also wore tight jeans that rode her hips and flared at the ankles. And red socks. Big, heavy, bright-red socks.

The sweater made things easy. No problem at all to slip his hands under there, to touch her bare skin, which was warm and so incredibly smooth. She shivered—and then she sighed.

They went on kissing. Her mouth invited him. Her slim, soft body pressed close.

He caressed the silky skin at the small of her back, followed the bumps of her spine upward. He already knew that she wore no bra. No red-blooded male could miss that, pressed as close as she was. Still, it was a delight to discover the fact all over again with his hands.

The sweater was in his way. He took the bottom of it and gave an upward tug. She helped him, lifting her arms. They had to break the kiss when the sweater got to their lips. But not for long. He pulled it over her head and tossed it behind him and pressed his mouth to her mouth again, gathering her close, feeling her tremble a little, smiling to himself.

In their time here together, he'd come to understand her—maybe better than she really wanted him to. Jilly had it all figured out—except when it came to herself. She was very tender at heart. Woundable.

He cupped her face again, made her look at him. "I won't hurt you, Jilly." He said the words and then he wondered why he'd said them. If he really meant to be certain of not hurting her, he shouldn't be doing what he was doing now.

Sex in the new millennium might not carry all the freight it once had. But there was still plenty of baggage around it. You got naked with someone and it could end up opening doors, setting off charges neither of you had expected. It could blow up in your face, and anybody who said they could guarantee otherwise was either a liar or a fool.

Jilly swallowed and nodded, her eyes wide. Wounded already. And sweetly dazed with desire. And right now, well, he was throwing good sense out the window and not caring in the least.

He wanted her. A lot. And her smooth, slim body was his for the taking.

He kissed her some more, daring to cup her small breasts, to play with the nipples, feel them pebble and harden. He pulled free of her mouth, only to kiss that wonderful chin of hers, to scrape his teeth on the stubborn tip of it, to slide his tongue along the satin skin of her throat.

There, he paused. He pressed his lips to the side of her neck, down low, just above the rise of her collarbone. He opened his mouth enough to draw on the thin, tender skin of her throat, sucking it against his teeth, raking it with his tongue. He would a leave a mark, and he knew it. He didn't care.

And neither did she, it seemed. She arched her throat to him eagerly. He eased the hard, drawing kiss, made it brushing, tender...

She said his name, on a whimper. He liked that, the sound of his name from her mouth while he kissed the bruise he'd brought up on her throat.

He kissed his way downward, capturing one pretty, hard little nipple and sucking it into his mouth. She moaned and he sucked harder, slipping a hand down, finding the buttons at the front of her jeans and releasing them, one by one.

He slid his hand in there, under the elastic of her silky little panties. Yes. Wet. Creamy. So good....

It had been such a long time since he'd felt that. The silky curls, the soft mound, the wet readiness, growing wetter at his touch.

He cupped her, and then dared to slide a finger into that waiting wetness, to rub the tiny, swollen nub while he continued to kiss her breast, to lick circles around the nipple, to close his mouth over it, to draw long and deep...

She was moving now, pushing herself against his hand, making sweet, hungry noises low in her throat, clutching his head to her breast. That gold-streaked brown hair dragged, feather-soft, against his cheek.

She whimpered his name again. And then again and again. Her movements grew more frantic. She held him closer, urging him to drink from her, while at the same time, below, she moved, riding his stroking hand.

And then it happened. She stiffened and cried out. He felt her release, the tender pulsing against his fingers, the spill of wetness, the hard shudder that ran through her and then the low, purring moan. She curved herself around him, sighing, her hair falling in a veil over his face.

He took his mouth from her breast and, very carefully, drew a long, steadying breath.

He was right at the edge, and it was taking all he had to keep from going over. The scent of her, the silky wetness against his hand, the way she had shuddered as she came, all that had swept him dangerously close to the breaking point.

"Oh," she said. "Oh, Will…" And she slid one soft hand down and laid it over his hardness, cupping him so lovingly.

It was too much. He lost it. He ground his teeth and held on tight as a shattering climax ripped through him.

Chapter 13

Aafter a minute or two, Will chuckled softly. Then he groaned. "You'd never guess, would you, that it's been a while for me?"

Jilly wanted to kiss him all over. She settled for lifting his face, cradling it tenderly and kissing his lips—a long, deep, wet, very thorough kiss.

When she finally pulled her mouth from his, she whispered, "We never even made it to a prone position. But I have to tell you, I feel just great."

"*Yet,*" he said low. "We haven't made it to a prone position *yet.*"

She really did like the way he said *yet.* "Ah. I stand corrected."

"You certainly do. And I think I need a towel."

A few minutes later, they went upstairs to the bed they'd slept in beneath their separate afghans just two nights before. Jilly got the condoms from her suitcase and set them on the table by the lamp. Then she took off the rest of her clothes. Will took his clothes off, too, and put them on the straight chair in the corner of the room.

She gulped when he came toward her, so fine and strong, with those wonderful broad shoulders and powerful arms—and ready for her all over again.

When he reached her, he wrapped his arms around her, but not tightly, just resting them, clasped, at the small of her back. Below, she could feel him, nudging her belly, causing that giddy lightness in her chest, that wonderful weakening at the knees—and that delicious melting sensation within.

He kissed the tip of her nose. "Who would have thought it—the two of us, together like this?"

She felt a smile break across her face. "Well, Caitlin, of course."

The corners of his mouth turned down in a frown— but a playful one. "You *would* have to remind me."

"You know what I think she needs?"

"Hit me with it."

"A new boyfriend."

He considered, then nodded. "It's a thought. She obviously needs more leisure-time activities. But on the other hand, I have to say…" He brushed a finger up and down her spine, leaving lovely goose bumps in his wake.

Jilly sighed and almost forgot what they were talking about. But then she saw the teasing gleam in his eyes. She asked, "You have to say what?"

"Well, if it hadn't been for Caitlin, you wouldn't be here now."

"Too true." She could top that. "And neither would you—in the most basic sense."

"You have a point. It's one I should probably try to keep in mind whenever I get that urge to do her serious bodily harm. She was, after all, the one who carried me around for nine months, the one who gave birth to me and then fed me and clothed me until I was old enough to do it for myself."

"And loved you. You know she did—she *does*—in her own unusual way."

"Yeah." His voice was rough—and tender, too. "You're right. I know she does."

Jilly looked up at him, thinking that she'd never felt quite this way before—and then thinking, Omigod, what am I *thinking*?

She did have to watch herself. She could end up in big trouble.

I've never felt this way before was the kind of thing a woman tended to think before she started telling herself she'd found her one and only—otherwise known as *a love for all time.*

And *a love for all time?*

Well, that was what Jilly had told herself she'd found when Benny came along.

And let us never forget where it ended with Benny: divorce court—and having to give a perfectly good bed to the Salvation Army.

Therefore.

If perhaps it was true that she'd *never felt this way before,* she was not moving on to believing that this just might be *a love for all time.*

It wasn't. It was a love for this moment. This magical, wonderful, tender, sweet moment. And for this moment, she was going to enjoy herself. Thoroughly.

She whispered, "Happy birthday, Will."

And he nodded, dark lashes low and lazy over those matchless blue eyes. "It is. One of the best. Maybe *the* best."

Now, that did sound lovely. But did she buy it? "Be honest, now. Nothing could top the year you got Snatch."

"This is pretty damn close—and you're not going to start in on me again about how I should get myself a pet, are you?"

"I never said you should get yourself a pet."

"Admit it. You thought it."

She fluttered her eyelashes at him. "Well, all right. Now that you mention it, I do think that a pet would be good for you."

"Now that *I* mention it?"

"You did bring it up, Will."

He made a low, disbelieving noise.

Which forced her to insist, "You did. You brought it up. You said—"

"I'm not going to argue with you, Jilly. I'll never win."

She smiled then. "Now you're learning."

"You know just what I need, huh?"

"Hmm," she said.

"Hmm, what?"

"Nothing. Just hmm…" She laid her hands against his chest, where silky hair grew in a T pattern, across and then down in a trail to his navel—and below. With a sigh, she let her eyes drift shut. "Nice. The feel of your heartbeat..."

His fingers had gone wandering again. He was tracing little circles up the curve of her back. "Am I going to live?"

"Oh, I think so. Your heart is very strong. A good, even beat." She teased the small, tight masculine nipples, rubbing them lightly with her flattened palms. "You'll live a very long time. And you'll be happy."

"You not only give advice, you tell fortunes?"

She slid her index finger down that tempting trail of hair in the center of his chest, over his stomach, his navel...

He gasped as she encircled him.

"Yes," she said, gasping a little herself. "It's true. I can see the future. I have...connections in the spirit world." She thought of Mavis, shivered, put that thought away.

He tightened his arms around her. His eyes had changed. The teasing light was gone. He groaned. "Kiss me, Jilly...."

She was stroking him—long, slow strokes. He felt so silky, so hot, so good.

His mouth closed on hers. Jilly kissed him eagerly, hungrily. She was thinking in a dazed, half-formed way that she wished this pleasure could go on forever, wished the plow would never come, the snow would never melt. That it would be just the two of them, snowbound for eternity, warm and close, naked together.

They fell across the bed, arms and legs all tangled up, in another of those endless, bone-melting kisses. When at last they broke for air, she tried to slither down his body, to taste him in the most intimate, encompassing way.

He laughed—a laugh that got caught on a needful groan. "No, you don't." He took her arm and pulled her up so they were face-to-face again. "You'll finish me, like you did in the kitchen. I'm not letting that happen this time."

"But—"

"No." He put a finger to her lips and he whispered, "I want to be inside you...."

And she felt his other hand, moving down her body, finding the feminine heart of her, parting her. She cried out and pushed her hips toward him, eager and ready for the pleasure he would give.

"So wet," he murmured against her hair. "So sweet..."

She made a low, urgent sound—of agreement, of excitement, of yearning. Of joy.

And then he rolled away from her. She let out a whimper, a tiny cry of need and loss. But in no time he was close again, with one of the condoms she'd left on the table. He quickly unwrapped it. She reached out, helped him slide it down. And then he was rising above her, slipping a knee between her thighs.

The old bed creaked in complaint at all the activity—not that either of them cared in the least.

She looked up at him, braced on his hands, staring down at her, the whole wide sky right there, in his eyes. A sky she was falling through, endlessly, joyfully.

She felt him, a touch of silky hardness, at her thigh and then right there, where she wanted him.

Needed him.

He came into her slowly, by aching, sweet degrees. She burned where he touched her. She went up in flames. Inside and outside, it was all one.

And she was falling, forever falling, through the endless blue depths of his eyes.

It was dark and they were still in the bed, though they'd crawled under the covers by then, when Jilly's phone rang. They looked at each other. And then they both laughed.

Jilly reached over and picked it up.

"Darlin' girl, let me speak to the birthday boy."

"Hold on." Jilly punched the Mute button. "You'll never guess who."

"Why didn't she call me on my own phone?"

"You want me to ask her?"

He swore and sat up. "Give it here." She handed it over. "What?" He listened. "Yeah?" He was silent. Caitlin, as usual, must be holding forth.

Jilly dragged herself to a sitting position, raked her love-ravaged hair out of her eyes and winked at Missy, who sat on the end of the bed giving herself a leisurely bath.

At last, Will said, "All right, Ma. Thanks." He pushed the end button and handed Jilly her phone.

She set it back on the table. "Let me guess. She wanted you to know how much this day means to her, the day you came into her life. She may not have always told you this, but she loves you with all of her heart and she's so grateful that you are her son."

He made a growling sound. And then he smiled. "Believe it or not, you're right. More or less."

"In her own words, of course."

"Of course. She also said I should be gentle with you, that you're a sweet, shy girl at heart."

She dipped a hand under the covers and ran her fingernail up his beautifully muscled hairy thigh. "She must be talking about some other girl you had up here once."

He held her gaze. "I never had any other girl up here. Only you, Jilly."

She thought, *Not even Nora?* But somehow, she didn't quite have the nerve to ask. Nora seemed, somehow, a special being. His one true love, lost forever, but forever in his heart....

She cut her eyes away—and then looked back, grinning. "And really, you didn't even have me up here on purpose, now did you?"

He didn't grin back. "Not at first, no. But now, as far as I'm concerned, I've got you here on purpose. I'm glad you're here, Jilly. Very, very glad."

She didn't know what to say to that. She felt...revealed, somehow. And that made her just a little bit nervous.

He seemed to understand, because suddenly he turned teasing. "Is that your stomach I hear growling?"

She laughed and put her hand on her tummy. "And here I thought it was an earthquake. Pass me the Cheez Doodles."

"Uh-uh. Let's go down and raid the refrigerator."

Right then, she remembered what she'd forgotten to do. "Oh, Will. I never baked your cake."

"As if I noticed."

"I could still do it. Why not? It's not like there's anything else we just have to get done."

"Jilly, stop. The last thing we need around here is another dessert."

"You're not *too* disappointed?"

"I am not in the least disappointed." He grabbed her by the shoulders and kissed her. Firmly. "Now, is it all right if we eat?"

They threw on their clothes—well, Will did. Jilly put on everything but her red-fleece top. It was still downstairs on the floor where Will had tossed it when he whipped it off over her head. When they got down there, she picked it up, shook it out and pulled it on. They heated up what they wanted to eat, after which they sat at the table and didn't speak to each other until they both had empty plates.

Jilly pushed back her chair. Will started to rise, too.

"Sit right there."

"You are the bossiest woman." But he didn't try to get up again.

She took their plates to the sink. And then she went around turning off lights—all except the one overhead. That accomplished, she got out the chocolate pecan pie, which only had two slices missing from it and would do just fine for a stand-in birthday cake. She found a candle in the candle drawer and stuck it in the center of the pie. There were kitchen matches in the old-fashioned dispenser on the back of the stove. She struck one and lit the candle.

Will chuckled as she flew over to douse the one remaining light.

"No laughing," she commanded. "This is serious business."

"Ah. Forgive me."

"All right. Just this once."

She returned to the pie, scooped it up and marched solemnly toward him, singing the birthday song. She set the pie before him and she sang the song all the way to the end. When she was done, he looked up at her, candlelight casting the planes and angles of his fine face into sharp relief.

"Well, what are you waiting for?"

"I thought maybe you'd have more instructions for me."

"What instructions? You make a wish. You blow it out."

"Gotcha." He tipped his head to the side and furrowed his brow, making certain she'd understand that he was doing the wish part. Then he closed his eyes, drew in a breath and blew out the candle.

She turned on the light.

He looked her up and down. "You've still got your clothes on."

Now, what was that supposed to mean?

He took note of her puzzled expression. "You said make a wish."

She understood. And groaned. "You're kidding."

"Uh-uh. I'd like you to do it now."

"You are getting awfully pushy."

"We're trying to give me good birthday memories. One way to do that is by seeing that my birthday wish comes true."

"Me naked? That's your birthday wish?"

He nodded.

"You should wish for something you haven't already had."

"Jilly. It's *my* wish. I think you should be nice and grant it." As if she could refuse him when he was looking at her like that. "And Jilly...."

"What?"

"Do it slowly, okay?"

After she finished her striptease, Will shoved back his chair, grabbed her and lifted her high against his chest. She squealed in surprise and then wrapped her arms around his neck and tucked her head into the curve of his shoulder. "You didn't eat your birthday pie."

"Later for that." He strode boldly across the cracked linoleum of the kitchen floor and up the stairs.

It was a long, heavenly night. They made love and they dozed, they woke up and talked for a while, shared a bag of Cheez Doodles, made love some more.

Very, very late, Jilly woke and could have sworn she saw Mavis at the foot of the bed—not reaching out, not floating toward her. Just standing there, a soft smile on her wrinkled face.

But maybe not.

When Jilly blinked, Mavis was gone. Jilly reached

for Will and her hand met warm, solid flesh. He opened his eyes, lazily murmured her name.

She whispered, "Kiss me?"

He answered by opening his arms.

In the morning, after breakfast, Jilly told him she really had to spend some time on her column. So he kissed her and went out to shovel snow.

By a little before one in the afternoon, she had four days wrapped up, pieces she'd been working on that just needed a decent concluding paragraph or a snappy intro. She zipped them off. That put her well ahead of schedule. She wouldn't have to get anything more in until after New Year's, which made her feel very smug and self-satisfied.

And how was Will doing outside? A delicious shiver slid through her and warmth pooled low in her belly, just at the thought of getting out there and shoveling alongside him. She put her laptop away and rolled her shoulders, which were a little bit achy from the shoveling she'd done yesterday. But not bad. Not bad at all. She threw on her coat and boots, gloves and hat, and went out through the kitchen door, detouring to the shed to grab the second shovel.

Out in the clearing, she discovered he'd made some serious progress. She couldn't even see him when she stood by the cars. She hurried along the path of frozen ground he'd made, toward the close clumps of brush and trees that lined the twisting driveway, aware of a sad, sinking feeling in her stomach, a dragging heaviness in her feet.

The time was coming, and it wouldn't be long now. Choices would have to be made—to go or to stay. And even if she stayed, how long would it last?

A few brief, lovely days. Then she'd return to her life and he'd go back to his. They'd meet periodically, for dinner at Jane's, a party at the Highgrade, some event in Las Vegas that Celia might organize.

Jilly's steps slowed to a stop at the top of the driveway. She looked down at the shovel in her hand. She wasn't going to like it much, having to be at get-togethers where Will would show up, too, where he'd smile and say hi, where they'd try to act normal and friendly, like casual acquaintances, after all that had happened here in the last few days. She had a feeling that was going to be pretty bad. Awful, even.

From somewhere far above, she heard a bird cry. Jilly lifted her head and sucked in a deep breath of bracing winter air. She could smell woodsmoke. And pine. She looked back at the old house, at the sparkling snow on the roof, the smoke from the chimney pipe trailing up toward the clear blue sky.

Winter in the mountains. Nothing like it in the world.

And as to her and Will…

Hey, the good part wasn't even over yet. She'd do well to remember that, to enjoy every last lovely second of the time they did have together. And who was to say that it had to end when they left this place? Okay, Will had told her that he wasn't in the market for a serious relationship. Did that mean there was some hard-and-fast rule that he could never change his mind?

People *were* allowed to change. And Will *had*

changed. They had both changed. Since they'd been snowed in here together, they'd gone from mutual dislike to friendship to becoming lovers.

Who could say what might happen next? Sometimes you just had to forge ahead and deal with whatever was around the next turn when you got there.

Jilly did forge ahead.

And around the next turn, from the bushes, a flicker of movement caught her eye.

It was a tail, wagging back and forth. The tail was hooked to a dog and the dog was staring right at her.

He was so *cute.* A brown-and-white shorthaired hound, nearly full-grown, but still with that soft, sweet puppy look about him. He had knobby, gangly legs and floppy ears and big, soft, lonely brown eyes.

But he was much too thin. His ribs stuck out.

"Oh, you little sweetheart…."

The dog let out a small, lonely-sounding whine, and then started backing deeper into the brush.

"Stay. Stay, boy. It's okay…."

The dog wagged his tail.

"Good boy." She took a step toward him.

The movement must have spooked him. He whirled and ran for the trees.

Jilly dropped her shovel and went after him, plunging hip-deep in just-cleared snow as soon as she stepped beyond the path Will had made. Ahead of her, at the edge of the brush where the trees started, the dog had paused to look back at her, tail low, but still wagging—hopeful, but not quite sure if he ought to trust her.

"Hey," she said softly, holding out her hand, palm up. "Come on. It's all right."

The dog perked those silky brown ears, tipped his sweet head to the side and whined again.

Jilly dared to haul her booted foot up and put it down into the knee-deep snow beyond the shoveled pile. Another step. And then another.

The dog whined once more and took off.

"Wait! Here boy, it's okay...." Jilly pushed on, snapping bushes aside, plowing through the snow. Behind her, she heard Will call her name.

But she didn't turn. She staggered on. She knew the dog was the animal she'd spotted yesterday and the day before, the shy creature she'd seen skirting the clearing. The poor guy was hungry. The poor guy needed help.

At last she reached the trees, where the snow was patchier than in the bare brush, making it easier to struggle ahead. But the tall pines not only made the way clearer, they also cut off the sun. Jilly shivered at the sudden drop in temperature—and kept going, fast as she could, following the tracks the dog had left, though by then the animal itself was nowhere to be seen.

From behind her, Will called again. "Jilly! Jilly, stop!"

She turned to look for him and saw him, just ducking under the thick cover of the trees. She waved at him, but kept on moving. She just wasn't ready yet to give up on the poor, lost mutt.

It was a big mistake—that she turned to wave and took her attention off the ground before her. She compounded the error by spinning quickly to the front again, rushing ahead without really looking where she was going.

It was one of those slow-motion moments. She put her foot down just as she registered that she'd stumbled onto a ravine. She tried to yank her foot back.

Too late.

She teetered. Gravity won.

With a sharp, startled cry, she fell, rolling. And then she hit her head on something hard. Lights seemed to pop and flash before her eyes. She was still rolling…

And then everything went black.

Chapter 14

Will had tried to warn her. He'd shouted at her to stop. He should have known that wouldn't work. Jilly, after all, was one of those women who could be counted on *not* to do what a man told her to do.

She went over. It was terrible to watch. She was there, twenty yards in front of him—and then she toppled from view into the ravine his grandmother had always called the Dead Drop, the one that seemed to be there out of nowhere if you didn't know to look for it.

Will raced for the spot where she had vanished, his heart beating out a rhythm of doom, her name a desperate litany scrolling through his brain.

Jilly, Jilly, Jilly, Jilly...

At last he reached the edge. He looked down. She was at the bottom. Curled in a ball.

Not moving.

He swore, a harsh string of very bad words. And then he started down, sliding, stumbling, almost falling, keeping his feet by some dark miracle, willing her to be all right.

Maybe two-thirds of the way, he lost his footing and went rolling. Fine, he thought, perfect. It would get him to her faster.

He hit the bottom and crashed to a stop against the trunk of a tree. With a groan, he surged to his feet. He'd landed close. Good. Two steps and he was standing over her.

"Jilly…" He knelt beside her and reached out, oh-so-carefully smoothing the hair, sticky with blood, away from her forehead.

And there it was, another bump, rising on the left side, exactly opposite the one she'd acquired the other night. It was bleeding, but not too badly. If he hadn't been so starkly terrified for her, he might have smiled.

She wouldn't like it, another bump like that. The good news was it didn't appear that any of the blood had gotten on her coat this time.

He was not a man who prayed—but he did then. He prayed that she would come to, look at him, for God's sake, that she was going to be okay. He prayed and he tried not to think that it was Christmastime, that bad things—the worst things, the horrible, ugly things— always happened at Christmastime.

"Jilly…" Very gently, smoothing more hair out of the way, he put two fingers at the side of her throat.

Yes! A pulse—a strong and steady pulse.

And right then she groaned and batted his hand away,

sucking in a deep breath, which caused her to groan again. She touched her head, whimpered, and rolled to her back, groaning some more as she did it, her sweet face scrunched up in an expression that told him rolling over had not felt good.

He ripped off his coat, wadded it in a ball and gently eased it beneath her head.

She moaned some more and touched the new injury a second time. "What...?" Her eyes popped open as she pulled her hand away enough to see the blood on her fingers. "Oh, no. Not again...."

"Jilly. Jilly, can you hear me?"

She blinked, focused on him, blinked again. "Will?"

"Yes. That's right. It's me, Will."

She lifted her head, looked around, then let it drop back to the pillow of his jacket again. "What happened?"

She knew who he was. She knew she'd been injured. What she'd said when she saw the blood on her hand led him to believe she even remembered that a tree branch had dropped on her a few nights ago.

The tight bands of dread and terror that had clamped around his chest eased a little. He realized he'd hardly been breathing and let himself suck in a long, hungry gulp of freezing winter air.

"Jilly, you fell. Into a small ravine not far from the driveway at my grandmother's house."

"I fell?" She was scrunching up her face again. And then her eyes widened. "I remember. There was a dog. Oh, Will. He was the sweetest thing. The way he looked at me, through those big, soulful brown eyes. I just loved him on sight, I swear I did."

What the hell was she babbling about? He couldn't begin to guess. "Listen. Concentrate."

"Concentrate," she repeated, as if the meaning of the word eluded her. Those heavy brows drew tightly together and she squinted up at him. "All right. What?"

"Are you hurt anywhere else, other than where you hit your head?"

"Oh, come on. I hurt *everywhere*."

He chuckled at that, though the sound had a frantic, strangled quality to it. "I know you do, sweetheart. What I mean is, do you think anything's broken or sprained?"

She closed her eyes. For several seconds she was very still. Then, slowly, she moved her head from side to side.

"Is that a no? Are you giving me a no?"

She made a low noise in her throat. "Yes, Will. I am giving you a no. I don't think anything's broken. Or even sprained. I honestly don't. I think that I have bruises on my bruises and it's not going to be fun to drag myself out of here. But I'm okay." And then she smiled. He'd never in his life been so grateful to see a woman smile. "Hey, pretty good, huh? I roll down the side of a rocky ravine and the worst I get is another whack on the head. Do I lead a charmed life, or what?" She started to sit up.

"Uh-uh. Better not." Gently but firmly, he guided her back down. "Rest a few more minutes."

"It's cold out here. I'm not lying out here for long, I'm warning you—and where's your jacket? You've got to be freezing." She frowned, felt behind her head. "Oh. Here it is. I want you to—"

"Jilly, damn it. Lie still."

"But you need your—"

"I'm fine. I don't want my coat."

"You don't have to shout."

She was right. She was hurt and the last thing she needed was to hear him barking orders at her. "Sorry. Just...keep the coat. Please."

"I won't lie here forever."

"Just for a few minutes."

"Oh, all right." She closed her eyes—for maybe thirty seconds. Then they popped open again. "Where's my hat? I'm not wearing my hat."

"I'm sure it's on the hillside somewhere. We'll find it. Relax."

She sighed. "Will?"

"Yeah?"

"Did you see the dog?"

She was back to the mysterious dog again. He shook his head.

She insisted, "There was a dog. Honestly. The cutest thing. Brown-and-white spotted. Shorthaired. I'm sure it was the animal I saw before—remember, yesterday when we were shoveling, and then also Christmas Day when we—"

"I remember."

"He looked so sad and hungry."

"You're saying you were chasing a dog just now?"

"Um-hm. But I lost him. He disappeared into the trees."

The last thing she needed to worry about at this point was some stray mutt. "Well, the dog is gone now."

"There were tracks. I'm sure if you—"

"Jilly. Are you listening?"

"I hate it when you treat me like I'm brain-dead."

"Forget the dog."

"But—"

"Please. Forget the dog."

She looked at him with the dangerous gleam of impending mutiny in her eyes. "I just think—"

"Please."

Finally, she sighed. "All right. I'll forget the dog. For now."

"Thank you."

Gingerly, she poked at the new lump on her forehead again. "Ugh. I do not believe this. One lump on each side." She shivered. "And I'm cold. *You* must be freezing." She lurched to a sitting position so fast, he didn't have time to make her stay down. "Ow. It hurts to sit up."

"I could have told you that."

"But it's manageable." She was already drawing her legs under her.

He grabbed her shoulder. "No, you don't."

She batted at his hand. "Oh, stop that. I'm fine. And we can't hang around down here all day. We'll freeze to death."

"You really believe you can make it back up that hill?"

"What else is there to do?"

"You can stay here. I'll go up and get—"

"Forget it."

"You didn't let me finish."

"You don't need to finish. You already said the part I don't like, which is that I would stay here."

"It's only until I can—"

"No way. I can make it. I know I can."

She seemed pretty sure of herself. And if she got a few steps and realized she'd overestimated her current capabilities, they could always do it his way. "All right. Let's go."

She flashed him a big smile to show how game she was. "Give me a hand, will you?"

He slid in close and she wrapped her arm over his shoulder. "Ready?" he asked.

"As I'll ever be."

"Here we go." He levered her upright.

She groaned, but she got there. "Oh, my poor head is spinning…."

"Want to lie back down?"

"Not on your life. Put on your coat and let's go." She looked so damned adorably determined.

He warned, softly, "I'll have to let go of you to do that. You'll have to stand on your own."

"Got that. Let's try it." Her cheeks were bright red and so was her nose. Her breath came out as a white cloud. Her forehead looked like a topographical map. He'd never seen anyone so beautiful in his life.

She nudged him with her hip. "Hey."

"Yeah?"

"You're still holding on."

He was. It had just occurred to him that he didn't want to let go. Ever.

Now, how the hell had that happened? It wasn't *supposed* to happen. This was an interlude they were sharing, wasn't it? Something sweet and passionate, tender—and temporary. She was helping him with his Christmas issues and they had become lovers. For a time.

He'd given up thinking about how they'd deal with what had happened between them when it was over. Maybe he'd been avoiding thinking about that. But one thing he'd been sure of. This wasn't going to be permanent.

So why, he wondered, was it suddenly so damn difficult to imagine letting go?

"Will? Are you all right?"

"Yeah. Fine." He stepped away from her.

She wobbled a little, but then she pulled it together. "See?" Her smile was smug now. "What did I tell you?"

He scooped up his jacket. "Okay, let's start climbing."

She stumbled more than once on the way up. But she didn't complain about it. She just went to all fours until she found her footing again. Whenever he offered a hand, she waved it away.

"Fine so far," she told him, and "I can do it," and "I'm okay. Really." And she was, as far as he could see. She was doing just fine.

She found her hat about halfway up. "You were right." She beamed him one of her beautiful smiles. "Here it is." She shook off the snow and pulled it on her head.

At the top, she let out a big breath. "Whew." She looked down to where they had been. "We made it." And then she veered off to the left.

He caught up with her in two strides and grabbed her

arm. "Not that way," he said gently and tried to turn her toward the driveway.

"Will, look." She pointed at the snow, at a set of animal tracks leading along the rim of the ravine. "The dog."

"What about it?"

"He went that way. We can follow him and maybe we'll find him, after all."

He wanted to shake her. And he wanted to protect her. And the desire to grab her and hold her and never let her go seemed to keep getting stronger as each minute ticked by.

"Come on. Let's find him." She tried to shrug off his grip.

He held on. "Listen to me."

"You know, you're squeezing my arm really hard."

He loosened his grip, but he didn't let go. "Say that we caught up with the dog."

"Okay, great. Say we did."

"If we caught up with the dog, then what?"

She looked at him, so hopeful, so determined, her forehead all bumps and bruises, blood in her hair. "We would bring him back to the house."

"How? The animal wouldn't come to you before. What makes you think it's going to be different now?"

"Well, but we can't just—"

"You've been hurt. The last thing you should do right now is to go trooping off into the woods after a stray dog."

"But what if he meets up with a mountain lion, what if he—"

"Jilly." He took her by the shoulders and turned her so she faced him fully. "You can't save every stray creature that runs across your path."

She glared at him. "I can try, damn it."

He cast about for the words that would get her to do what was best for her. "Look. You said you think this dog was the same animal you've seen twice before."

"I know it is."

"Then have a little damn faith, would you? The dog's lasted this long. Maybe it knows what it's up to. And there *are* other houses in these mountains. It probably belongs to someone who lives in one of them."

"But he was so skinny. And he didn't have a collar…." Her mouth twisted. She looked up at him, pleading with her eyes. He refused to give in. At last she let out a long sigh. "All right. I'll go inside."

He barely had time to enjoy his relief before he realized there was a bargain coming.

"But," she said.

"Hit me with it," he muttered bleakly.

"*I'll* go on inside. *You* follow the tracks and see if you can find him."

No damn way. Now she'd managed to get out of that ravine, he wasn't taking his eyes off her until he was certain she was going to be all right. She must have picked that up from his expression, because she came up with another idea.

"Well, then, how about this? We'll go in together. I'll behave myself for a while. You'll see that, once again, I have escaped the looming specter of brain damage."

"Brain damage is nothing to joke about—and how long is a while?"

"An hour."

He scowled at her.

She offered, "Two?"

He said nothing.

Her mouth went tender—and her eyes knew way too much. "Oh, Will. I know you're scared. Since it's Christmastime, of course you're expecting the worst. But it's not going to happen. I'm going to be fine. How about this? I'll do what you said. I'll have some faith that the dog will survive another day. But then, tomorrow morning, when it's been over twelve hours and I'm still fine, we'll go out together. We'll see if we can find him."

It was all these damn conflicting emotions that were doing him in. She'd been hurt and he wanted to take care of her. But she wouldn't let him take care of her. She wanted to go traipsing off on a wild goose chase after some lost dog. And that made him want to shout at her. And then, he couldn't stop asking himself, how could any injured person be so damn sexy, standing there, shivering, at the edge of that ravine?

"What do you say?" she asked softly.

He swore. "All right. It's a deal." He grabbed her arm again.

And he refused to let go until they were back in the house.

Chapter 15

Jilly meant to be a model patient, she truly did. But she'd never been all that good at being sick even when she really *was* sick. There was just too much to do to waste time lying around getting well. And to have to rest and be still and try to be quiet when there was nothing wrong with her beyond a few bumps and bruises, well, it was a lot to ask.

But she'd made an agreement. And she would try to stick by it.

Will insisted on tending her injury. After she rinsed the blood from her hair, he made her stand by the sink while he used a pad dipped in peroxide to clean the bits of dirt and debris out of the abrasion that crowned her newest goose egg.

"Oops," she couldn't help teasing him, "looks like death by infection is outta here."

For that, she got a scowl and a grunt.

"Will you stop worrying?" she implored.

"Yeah. Eventually. For now, lie on the sofa. Rest."

"For how long?"

"Jilly, you promised you'd behave."

"I'm behaving. I just want to know how long I have to lie down."

"At least an hour."

"Oh, great. It's not bad enough I roll into a ravine. I have to lie down for an hour. You know I really hate that. Just lying there, with nothing to do."

He only looked at her, the way a put-upon parent might look at a recalcitrant child.

She asked, sheepishly, "So would you mind if I got my laptop first?"

"I'll get it." He had the ice pack all ready. He handed it to her. "You lie down."

Carefully, she pressed it to her left temple. "And bring both of the pillows from my bed, will you? The ones on the sofa are too skinny."

He was already at the stairs by then. He signaled he'd heard her with a wave of his hand.

Jilly trudged into the living area and plunked herself down on the edge of the sofa bed. She pulled the ice pack away and prodded her new bump a little. Then she put the pack to her temple again and looked at her heavy green socks for a while, noting the way her head pounded when it was lowered, acutely aware of all her new aches and pains—at her left hip, the small of her back, her right shoulder. Those areas would probably be black and blue by tomorrow.

She sighed. Oh, well, at least it was overcoat weather. To the world at large, the damage wasn't even going to show—well, except for the disaster that was her forehead. Hmm. Maybe what she needed was one of those slouchy Ralph Lauren straw hats.

She heard him coming back down the stairs. "Oh, thank you," she said, her heart melting a little when he appeared around the corner from the kitchen, carrying everything she'd asked for—and a bag of Cheez Doodles, too. He helped her to get comfy sitting up against the pillows, her snack beside her and her laptop on her knees.

The hour started out fairly well. She spent a few minutes fooling with her e-mail correspondence. But that was awkward, since one hand was occupied holding the ice pack in place. Next she went to the Web to get in a little research on a possible future column. But then she made the mistake of looking up.

Will sat in his easy chair, cell phone in hand, his face a grim mask. He stared straight at her, clearly awaiting the first sign of coma or convulsion so he could dial 911.

She laid the ice pack aside long enough to shut down her computer. "All right, Will." She set the laptop on the floor. "We need to talk."

He frowned. "About what?"

Where to begin? "I'm fine. Can't you see? Nothing terrible is going to happen to me. And all the progress you've made in the past few days is going to be worth exactly zip if you refuse to give up all these irrational fears."

His lip curled—and not in a smile. "Irrational."

"Don't sneer at me. I said your fears are irrational. And I think, if you'll examine them a little, you'll see that I'm right."

He sneered some more. "In the past five days—since you've been around me—you've had a tree limb fall on your head, your cat has disappeared, and you've fallen down a ravine."

She readjusted her ice pack. "So?"

"So, I don't like it. It gives me the creeps. It's as if I'm a jinx or something."

"Will Bravo."

"When you say my name like that, I know damn well a lecture is coming."

"Listen to me carefully. You are a reasonable man. And as a reasonable man, you have to know that there's no such thing as a jinx."

"Sure. I know that. It doesn't change the way I feel. And I feel that I'm a jinx. People and animals get hurt when they hang around me at Christmastime."

"Oh, that is crazy. You know that it is. You can't blame yourself because a branch breaks off a tree and falls on my head, because a cat runs out a door you didn't even leave open, because I don't look where I'm going and end up falling down a hill. None of those things was in any way your fault."

He set the phone on the chair arm. "Look. You're supposed to be resting, not arguing with me."

She was not getting through to him and she knew it. "Will, you're worrying me."

He made a low, growling sound. "*I'm* worrying *you?*"

"Yes. Oh, don't you see?" She waved the ice pack, a

wild gesture in the general direction of the tree they'd put up two days before. "We were tricked into being here, together, for the holiday. You despised me and I couldn't stand you. But look what happened? It's turned out so beautifully, in the end. We made a real Christmas, just the two of us. And you said yourself that yesterday was one of the best birthdays you've ever had."

Right now, he was saying nothing. He only stared at her, his jaw set and his eyes unreadable.

"Oh, Will, why not look on the bright side? Sometimes bad things happen, but on the whole, life is really something. You said it yourself, out there in the woods a little while ago. You just have to have a little faith. You have to trust, to believe that things will work out all right in the end."

"And what if they don't?"

"Well, then, you pick yourself up off the floor and you try again."

"And if trying again means that other people will get hurt or die?"

"Oh, listen to yourself. You can't possibly believe what you're saying."

She waited for him to tell her that she was right, of course he didn't believe such a crazy thing. But the seconds crawled by and he didn't answer. He only looked at her, stone-faced and brooding, like the doomed hero of some tragic nineteenth-century romance.

At last he shrugged. "You're right. It's not logical. Let's drop the subject."

"But—"

"Damn it, Jilly. I mean it. There's no point in talking about this."

Jilly looked down at her socks. There was something about the way he'd said *Damn it, Jilly* that let her know the subject was closed—for the moment, anyway.

Maybe later she could get him to talk about it some more.

She put the ice pack down, opened her bag of Cheez Doodles and held them out to him.

"No thanks."

So she took a handful for herself and picked up her laptop again. She worked for the remainder of the hour she'd promised to rest, crunching her cheese snack, taking care not to look up at him. She really didn't want to see him sitting there, watching her like a hawk, ready with gruff denials if she dared to suggest he ought to lighten up and stop waiting for her to keel over dead.

For the rest of the day, Will was tender, solicitous— and emotionally about a million miles away. Once he'd begun to believe that he wouldn't have to call in the paramedics after all, he dared to leave her alone long enough to go outside and put the shovels in the shed.

When he back came in, he looked at her probingly. "You're feeling all right?"

"I'm feeling great." It was a slight exaggeration—but in a good cause.

"Will you be okay on your own if I have a quick bath?"

"I'll be fine."

He was in and out of the bathroom in record time.

When he emerged, she was standing at the refrigerator trying to decide what to whip up for a very late lunch.

"You okay?" he demanded, as if he suspected she might have been temporarily comatose when he wasn't looking.

She bit back a flippant reply, shut the refrigerator door and sauntered over to him. He eyed her with a wariness she didn't find flattering.

However, nothing ventured, as the old saying went.

And he really was such a gorgeous example of the male gender. How could a girl resist? All shaved and smelling so clean and good. She put her arms around him and laid her head against his shoulder. Those strong arms encircled her and held on tight. For a minute, she almost dared to hope that things were going to be okay.

But then she lifted her head and tried to kiss him.

He took her by the forearms—and gently pushed her away. "What's to eat?"

So they ate. After that, he suggested a game of checkers. She almost said she'd prefer that they take off all their clothes and do naughty things to each other.

But no. A remark like that was a little too risqué for the mood he was in. He seemed to see her as an invalid who refused to admit she was sick. And he was hardly the kind of man who did naughty things to invalids.

She gave him her most cheerful smile. "I'd love to beat you at checkers."

She didn't. He won. Five times running.

When he took her last man for the fifth time, she wanted to demand a kiss as consolation for the trouncing she'd endured. But then she looked up from the checkerboard. He'd been watching her—and the minute she caught his eye, his gaze shifted away.

This was awful. It felt as if they were back at square one. They might never have been lovers, the way he looked at her now.

A new approach was needed. Maybe, since none of her attempts to get close to him seemed to work, she'd be better off to surrender the field for a while. Give him a little private time.

In fact, she could do with some private time herself. Some time to relax without the constant pressure of his worried gaze tracking her every move. Time to try to figure out how to bridge this chasm that seemed to have opened up between them.

He was putting the game away. She suggested, "I think what I could use is a long, hot bath."

"Help yourself."

In the bathroom, while the tub filled, she shucked off her clothes and examined all her bruises in the cracked mirror on the back of the door.

Ugh. Not a pretty sight. The one on her right shoulder was especially large and purple and shaped roughly like the continent of Africa. And her forehead was a mess. Aside from the gruesome bruising, she looked as if she was about to sprout a pair of horns.

Ah, well. She had no broken bones. Yes, it was ugly, but it wasn't *permanent* ugly. In a few weeks, it would all fade away.

And also, she did have one *good* bruise—the tiny one at the base of her throat, where Will had marked her with a passionate bruising kiss the first time they made love.

She climbed into the bath, shampooed and then gently washed her poor, battered body. After that, she lay back and drifted. She shut her eyes and drew in deep breaths, setting her mind on peaceful thoughts.

Until Will pounded on the door and she lurched upright, sending water sloshing everywhere.

"What!"

"Are you okay?"

"Fine."

"Are you sure?"

"Will."

"What?"

"If I'm about to die, I'll let you know."

"Is that supposed to be funny?"

"Go. Away."

A silence. Then she heard his footsteps moving off. She spread her wet washcloth over her face, sank back into the cooling water, and wondered what she was going to do about him.

It got worse.

He went to bed with her, yes. But she should have known what he was up to when he climbed between the covers wearing a T-shirt and sweats.

Determined to give it her best shot, she cuddled up close and lifted her mouth for a kiss.

She got a quick, dry peck.

"Goodnight, Jilly." He reached over and flicked off the light and settled in on the other pillow with his back to her.

She lay there, staring into the darkness. She was starting to get angry. "Will?"

He made the kind of noise that was probably supposed to make her think she was waking him up. Right. No way he was sleeping. He was lying there, listening, waiting for something terrible to happen to her so he could take steps to save her.

"You only came to bed with me to keep an eye on me, didn't you? If you weren't set on protecting me from whatever awful thing you're just sure is going to happen to me, you wouldn't be here now, would you?"

He sat up and turned on the light. "You want to fight, is that it?"

"No. I don't. I promise you, I don't."

"You sound like a fight just before it happens."

"I admit, I'm getting close. And you just avoided answering either of my questions."

He raked his hand back through his hair. "Jilly..."

She waited. But he didn't say anything else. Only her name in that sad, unfinished, trailing-off way.

"Are you going to talk to me, Will?"

"Sure. What do you want me to say?"

Be calm, she told herself. Do not start shouting at him. "You're just so far away. I don't know what to do, don't know how to get through to you."

There was a pause, endless and awful. Then he said, quietly, "Maybe you should just let it be." He sounded so...weary. So completely resigned.

Her anger fizzled and died.

She was tired, too. It had been a tough day. Right now, she simply didn't have the energy to keep struggling to scale the wall he'd put up between them.

Maybe tomorrow...

"I guess so," she said softly. He said nothing, so she whispered, "Turn off the light."

He reached for the lamp. The room went dark again.

They lay down, not touching, facing opposite directions. After a while, Missy jumped up between them and settled in, purring.

At least the cat's happy, Jilly thought. She closed her eyes. And for the first time, she actually found herself hoping for a visit from Mavis. She could certainly use a little advice from beyond the grave concerning what to do about Will.

When Jilly woke in the morning the only dream she recalled was a long, rambling one where she'd gone to a party of strangers. Once she realized she didn't know a soul at that party and no one wanted to talk to her anyway, she kept trying to leave. Too bad every door she opened only led to another room full of people she didn't know who had no interest at all in talking to her.

She could not remember seeing Will's grandmother in the dream. Where were the spirits of the dead when you needed them?

And where was Will? She reached out, touched the wrinkled sheet on his side of the bed. Cold.

She got dressed—moving a little stiffly due to her various bumps and bruises—and went downstairs. He was sitting at the table, eating his breakfast. He looked up and smiled at her, a friendly smile.

But cool. And distant. A smile that told her the wall between them was still firmly in place.

She had the most awful, hollow sort of feeling right then. She thought, *It's over. What we had is all we're going to have. He's going to get up and go outside and get the driveway cleared so that I can go.*

"Good morning," she said and smiled back at him. Then she made her instant coffee and poured herself some cereal.

He was done eating before she finished. He went into the bathroom. She heard the water running. When he came out, he headed straight for the coat rack and started putting on his boots.

"What's up?" she asked, her voice falsely bright.

He pulled on his jacket. "I'm going to get out there, get to work on the driveway."

Her heart felt as if some cruel hand had wrapped around it and was squeezing hard. Oh, yeah. He needed to get that driveway cleared. No way to get rid of her until he did.

And then she remembered that poor, lost dog. And Will's promise of the day before.

She said, "I'll be out in a few minutes. We can look for the dog."

He was on one knee, tying his bootlace. He glanced up. "Do you really think there's any point in that?"

"I don't know. I just want to try."

"I'd say it's pretty unlikely we'll find the animal now. You realize that, don't you?"

There was a traitorous tightness at the back of her throat. She came very close to hating herself for that, for the urge to shed her tears of hopelessness right there in front of him. "I just want you to keep the promise you made to me yesterday."

"Jilly…" There it was again. Her name. Trailing off into nothing. "Listen, I—"

"No." She swallowed, pulled her shoulders back. "*You* listen. If you don't want to look for the dog, fine. I'll look by myself." She had him there and they both knew it. No way he would let her go off by herself—except when she left him, which would be very soon now.

"All right," he muttered, rising. "I'll help you look for the dog." Instead of turning for the door, he went through the living area. He disappeared into his bedroom and when he came out, he had an old rifle with him.

She'd lived in the mountains as a girl. She knew that it was wise to have a weapon if you planned to traipse around deep in the woods. But they shouldn't be going that far from the house. "I don't think you'll need that."

"Maybe not. Better safe than sorry, though." He grabbed his gloves from the shelf above the coatrack and went to the door.

"Will. I'd like to make one other point, if you don't mind."

He paused with his hand on the knob. "Go ahead."

"Other than this, to help me look for that poor lost dog, I am not asking for anything you don't want to give. I don't *want* anything you don't want to give. Is that clear to you?"

"Perfectly." His voice was soft and utterly flat. He pulled open the door and went out, closing it quietly but firmly behind him.

A half an hour later, she got the second shovel from the shed and went to find him.

He was a good two-thirds of the way down the driveway. She felt it again—that infuriating tightness at the back of her throat. He looked so strong and purposeful, rhythmically shoveling, his hair gleaming bronze in the thin winter sunlight, working hard to clear the way for her to leave him.

He tossed a final shovelful off the driveway. Then he stuck his shovel in the high bank of cleared snow and turned to face her, panting slightly, a dew of sweat on his brow. "Ready?"

She stood her shovel a few feet from his. "I'll help you with the driveway once we've looked for the dog."

His gaze swept over her, from her battered forehead to the toes of her boots. "It's not necessary. I'm sure, after yesterday, you've got some serious aches and pains."

"I'm all right. A little exercise will loosen up the stiffness."

He looked as if he would argue, but then he pressed his lips together and gave her a curt nod. "Suit yourself. I left my rifle on the porch."

She resisted the urge to argue again that they didn't need a rifle. She knew it was an argument she'd never win. "I'll go with you."

They walked back to the house together. He got the rifle and they set off, Jilly in the lead.

"This way," she said, when she found the spot where she'd first seen the dog the day before. They slogged through the piled-up snow at the bank and then into the bare brush, following the tracks from yesterday, widening the path their own boots had already helped to flatten. Quickly, they reached the cover of the trees and soon after that, the edge of the ravine.

The dog's tracks were still recognizable. They followed them along the rim of the ravine for perhaps two hundred yards, and then away from the edge. Once, as they began to climb the hill behind the house, Jilly lost the trail. But she picked it up again several yards on. That happened a number of times. She'd lose the tracks only to find them a few minutes later. They were descending by then. After a time, they ended up on level ground once more. About then the tracks just petered out to nothing.

Jilly was still in the lead. She stopped beneath a tall cedar and admitted, "I don't know where to go from here. I can't tell where he went."

She expected Will to shrug, turn around and head straight for the driveway—wherever that was. She'd lost track by then of how to get directly to the place where they had started. However, she felt reasonably certain she could get them back to the ravine, and from there, retrace their steps along it until they reached the place where she had fallen. Once she got to that point, it should be a simple task to find the way back to the driveway through the trees.

But Will didn't do what she expected. "Over here."

He had picked up the trail. He took the lead and they were on the move again.

Maybe fifteen minutes later, she heard what she thought was water—a creek or even a river, rushing fast. But then they came out to the edge of a cliff—a high embankment, really. She looked down and saw the road below them. It was clear of snow. The whooshing of the cars going by made that sound that she'd mistaken for rushing water.

Will went to the edge. He was frowning. "Wait a minute."

She stayed there while he backtracked along the

route they'd just taken. When he returned to her, he was shaking his head. She knew what he'd tell her before he spoke.

"I'm sorry, Jilly. I've lost the trail. I don't know where to go from here."

She met his eyes then. "Neither do I."

He waited. She felt tenderness for him rising, soothing the hurt in her heart. He wanted to keep the one promise he'd made her. He had tried to keep it. But the dog was nowhere to be found.

And Will Bravo wasn't ready to love again. She had to accept that. It was time they both moved on.

She sent a brief prayer heavenward, that wherever that sweet, shy mutt might be by now, he was safe. And well.

And then she gave Will a real smile, one that was a little bit sad, but also one-hundred-percent sincere. "We haven't seen a single bear or mountain lion. I don't think you'll have to use that rifle of yours, after all."

He looked vaguely abashed. "You're right. I probably should have left it at the house. I'm a little on edge, that's all."

"Positive that some other bad thing is bound to happen?"

"You got it."

She opened her mouth to promise him that she was not allowing any more bad things to happen. But then she realized it would only be one more promise destined to remain unkept. Another bad thing *was* going to happen: the end of their time together. A hundred rifles couldn't protect them against that.

Jilly set her mind on the business at hand. "I'm completely turned around. I hope you can get us back to your grandmother's house."

He nodded. "No problem. This way." He began trudging through the snow along the rim of the embankment.

As they moved along the edge, the embankment sloped downward. About twenty minutes after they first came out above the road, they were walking on the shoulder, single-file, sticking close to the dirty ridge of snow pushed aside by the plow. Cars and trucks and SUVs, crusted with road salt, snow piled high and white on their roofs, rushed past them, sometimes too close for comfort.

They came around a curve and Will pointed at a narrow driveway that met the road and wound off into the trees maybe thirty yards ahead. "There. That's it."

Jilly stopped where she was. "The driveway to your grandmother's house?"

"That's right."

"But it's been cleared."

"The plow must have—" He cut the sentence off himself. There was no need to go on. As they watched, the snowplow emerged from the driveway. The driver turned onto the road and saluted them with a mittened hand as he rolled by.

They got their shovels and went inside.

"Well," she said, "Let's get that tree taken down."

He shook his head. "Leave it."

"I promised you I would—"

"Leave it. Please. I'll handle it myself."

"You're sure?"

"Positive."

An hour later, with Will's help, Jilly had taken the unneeded chains off her 4Runner and cleared the windshield of snow and ice. She'd packed up her stuff and stowed it in back. Missy was safe in her carrier, already complaining from the passenger seat.

Jilly made one more pass through the old house. But there was nothing she had left behind.

Well, maybe her heart. But, hey. She was a strong, self-reliant and self-directed woman. She knew her own worth and her single life was a good life. She had no doubt she'd get over Will Bravo.

Eventually.

He went out with her to see her off. The sun was directly overhead by then, the sky ice-blue and clear.

They stood by the driver's door of her car and looked at each other for longer than they should have.

He was the one who broke the silence. "You know I'm going to miss you." It wasn't a question. He added, low and rough, "I'm going to miss you really bad."

She knew exactly what he meant. But she couldn't have said a word right then if her life and his life and Missy's life depended on it. So she swallowed and she nodded and she found her throat had loosened up enough that she could speak, after all.

"What I'd like to hear you say right now is that next year you'll be with your family when Christmas comes around."

He stuck his hands in his pockets and looked down at his boots. "I'll work on it, Jilly."

It wasn't the answer she'd hoped for. But it was something. And she might as well put a good spin on it. She sucked in a big breath of freezing air and let it out in a rush. "Well, okay. What more could I ask?"

Lots more. And they both knew it. But there was no point in asking for what you weren't going to get.

"Goodbye, Will." She turned to reach for her door.

Before she got it open, though, she heard him swear low. And then he was grabbing her by the arm, spinning her back around to him and yanking her close.

He looked down into her startled face, his eyes blue shards, two flags of color staining his beard-roughened cheeks. And then his mouth swooped in and closed on hers.

It was the kiss of her dream.

The one that burned her lips right off.

His hands ran down her back, pressing her close to him so she could feel how much at least one part of him wanted her to stick around. She kissed him back, as hard and hungrily as he was kissing her.

And then he pulled her closer still, so close that the savage kiss was broken. They breathed together. She could hear his heart beating, right in time with her own. Twin tears slid down her cheeks. She moved her head just a fraction, enough to wipe them away on his jacket, so he would never have to know they had fallen.

From some unknown reserve she hadn't realized she possessed, she found the strength to pull away. Still held in his arms, she looked up at him.

"This isn't going to be one of those steamy relationships that never really goes anywhere, but doesn't quite go away, either, is it?"

He gave her that wonderful, wry smile of his. "No. I swear to you. It was only that it hit me all over again. You're really going. And I couldn't stand it, not without one final kiss."

"So when we see each other—and you know we will—at Jane and Cade's, or the Highgrade, or at Celia and Aaron's, or maybe just coincidentally, on the street..."

He made a low sound in his throat. "I get the picture. Smile. Say hi. Walk on by."

"It probably won't be a whole lot of fun."

"I hear you. But we'll manage it."

"And right now, you'd better let go of me."

He released her. Damn. She hated that.

"Do me one last favor?" he asked, so softly.

"Anything." And she meant it.

He took her hand, turned it over and folded a piece of paper into her palm. "That's my cell phone number. Call me when you get home. I just want to know that you made it safely."

She snatched both hands behind her back—quickly. Or else she would have reached for him. "Oh, Will. How can I convince you I'm going to be just fine?"

"Just call."

"All right."

She forced herself to turn again, to grab the door handle and pull the door wide. She hitched herself up and slid behind the wheel, setting the scrap of paper with his phone number on it in the little niche beneath the ashtray and hooking her seatbelt in place.

Will shut her door for her. He stepped back, mouthed, "Drive carefully," at her through the window.

She gave him a jaunty wave, started up her car and headed down the driveway, taking extreme care not to allow herself so much as one glance back at him, or the clearing, or the old house where she'd found love so unexpectedly—and then, just as suddenly, lost it again.

Chapter 16

Jilly got home without incident. She dialed the number Will had given her as soon as she pulled beneath her carport and turned off her car.

He answered midway through the first ring. "Jilly?"

She ached for him, picturing him in his easy chair, the phone in his hand, driving himself a little nuts with his usual expectations of disaster as he waited for her call. "I'm here. I'm fine."

"Thank you."

"Goodbye, Will."

She heard a click and the line went dead.

Jane called her on her cell the next day. "Well, are the roads cleared?"

It took Jilly a second or two to realize that Jane assumed she was still at the old house high up in the mountains. "Yes, they are. As a matter of fact, I'm home."

Silence echoed down the line as Jane digested that piece of information. "Home? In Sacramento?"

"That's right."

"But I thought you said you would call me before you left, maybe come on in to New Venice and stay with Cade and me until New Year's."

Jilly cast about madly for a way to explain herself. Nothing came to mind except the truth, which was a long story with an unhappy ending and would entail spilling the beans about Will—something she really didn't want to do. She and Will were nobody's business. They'd had a beautiful time together and now it was over and telling his sister-in-law all about it wouldn't help the situation one bit.

Jane prompted, "Jilly?"

At a loss for what to say, she found herself launching into a verbal tap dance. "Oh, that's right. I did say I'd call. I'm sorry, it's just that something came up. I had to get home."

Jane cleared her throat, pointedly. "Jillian. Please. I've got my bull-detector set on you and it is beeping. Fast and loud. What's going on?"

"I just wanted to come home, that's all."

"You mean that whatever it is, you're not going to tell me."

Jilly wondered what could have possessed her to try being evasive with Jane. With Jane, it was always better to come right out with it when you didn't intend to tell her something. Jane could get ugly if you lied to her.

"You're right, Janey. I'm not going to tell you."

"Was it Will? Did he—?"

"Will was a perfect gentleman. I just wanted to come home."

"Celia said he told you all about poor Nora. Evidently, he gets very weird over the holidays."

"We worked everything out. We had a fine time." Oh, yes they had. They really had. "And I'm very sorry I didn't call you. It was rude. I just had a lot of things on my mind."

There was another silence—but not such a strained one as before. "There's no need to apologize. You know that. I only wish you would tell me what's bothering you."

"I'm all right, Janey. Truly."

"You sure you won't change your mind and come on up to visit, anyway? We would love to see you."

No, you wouldn't.

Jilly was standing by the brass-framed mirror in her apartment's small entrance hall and what she saw reflected there wasn't anything anybody else needed to see. She'd stopped for gas at a convenience mart yesterday and made the mistake of going inside. The clerk had looked up from the register and gasped.

"My God, lady. Are you okay?"

That was when Jilly decided she'd avoid leaving her apartment for a while—until the bruises went away and the bumps went down or until something came up where she had no choice. And if she did go out, she'd have sense enough to wear a hat pulled low on her forehead.

"Jilly? What do you say? Why don't you come on up?"

"Thanks bunches, Janey. But I just can't make it right now."

They said goodbye a few minutes later. Jilly punched the button to end the call and then had to stop herself from dialing Will's number. It was a problem she had now. Every time she had a phone in her hand, her fingers just itched to call him.

She'd torn up the paper with his number on it and flushed the pieces down the toilet. But that hadn't helped. Somehow, that number had managed to burn itself into her brain. She'd forget her own name before she'd forget that number.

Oh, what was she going to do with herself? Maybe she ought to sit down and write a letter to "Ask Jillian." She could give herself the answer to all her troubles and print it in her column.

Dear Jillian…

What? She didn't even know where to begin.

She put the phone down and went to make herself a double batch of Kraft macaroni and cheese. As she sat down to eat, she told herself she was not even going to think about what Will might be doing right now.…

Will had made himself a double batch of Kraft macaroni and cheese. He took his place at the table and picked up his fork and dug in.

A few minutes later, he realized he'd stopped eating. He was just sitting there, his food growing cold in front of him, staring at the kitchen door, wishing a certain gray-eyed woman with gold-streaked brown hair would come bursting through it, that mouth of hers going a mile a minute....

He picked up his fork again. He had to stop that, getting lost in thoughts of Jilly. She was gone and it was for the best.

He was just tired, that was all. He'd had a rough night last night, missing the warmth of her beside him.

And his dreams had been unsettling.

In one, he saw his grandma Mavis standing at the foot of the bed, shaking her head at him, her blue eyes so sad. And in another, he saw Nora, standing a long way off, in some misty nowhere place, waving, calling to him. But he couldn't make out what she said.

Both dreams had left him feeling bleak and depressed. And then he got up in the morning and went out to the living area and the first thing he saw was that damn tree of Jillian's. He couldn't take looking at that tree until New Year's.

So, before he even allowed himself a cup of instant cappuccino, he'd taken the thing down and tossed it out in back to chop up for firewood at some later date. He'd packed up all of Mavis's old decorations and put them where they belonged, in the crawl space upstairs.

And then, damn it, he found himself missing the tree after it was gone. He had this feeling of an empty space, there, by the window, where the tree ought to be.

Will shook his head. He forked up a mound of macaroni and cheese and shoved it into his mouth. He chewed, stolidly. Life was just that way sometimes, bad dreams and memories. Restless nights and lonely days.

Outside, it was near dark. The wind was up, whistling through the trees, making the old window frames rattle, whining at the door....

Will set his fork down again. He listened intently. That wasn't the wind.

Yes. There it was again. It sounded like...

Will got up and opened the door.

Jilly had had a couple of consultations scheduled for the first week in January. Friday, when she got home, she'd managed to reach those clients and move them both to a later date. Her column was no problem. She did that from home, anyway. She planned to really churn them out while she was stuck at home, estimating that by the time she was ready to show her face in public again, she'd be at least a month ahead. And that, as the divine Martha would say, was a good thing. In the end, the way Jilly saw it, everything had its upside— even hiding out in her apartment in order to spare other people the horror of having to look at her.

Saturday, a few hours after Jilly spoke with Jane, Caitlin called. Correction, Jilly thought, when she heard that low, sexy voice. *Almost* everything had its upside.

"Sweetie, I called Jane and I asked if she'd heard from you and she said that she'd talked to you and you were at home. I couldn't believe it. Tell me it isn't so."

"It's so, Caitlin. I'm at home."

"I don't get it. What the hell's the problem now?"

"There is no problem. Everything's fine."

"Where's Will?" Caitlin demanded, in a tone that seemed to hint that Jilly must have done something criminal with her middle son.

"The last I saw him, he was up at Mavis's place. I think he plans to be there until the second of January—and Caitlin, Will and I talked about you. We decided that what you need is to find yourself another boyfriend."

"Don't try to switch subjects on me, darlin' girl. When I want a new boyfriend, I'll find one. And when I go after information, I don't quit until I get it. Did you two have a tiff? Is that what you're telling me?"

"Caitlin, let me give it to you straight."

"Go right ahead. Hit me with it. I like it straight."

"There is nothing going on between Will and me. We're…friendly acquaintances. And that's all."

Caitlin made a snorting noise. "Well, that is a great big load of stinkin' you-know-what if I ever heard one."

"Caitlin. I have to go. Have a happy New Year." Jilly hung up and turned off the phone.

"Omigoodness, Jillian. What *happened?*" Jilly's neighbor, Orlene Findley, gaped at her, horrified.

Jilly had made the mistake of stepping out to get her Monday morning *Press-Telegram* without checking first to see if anyone was going to have the misfortune of getting a look at her. She'd just bent down to scoop up the paper when Orlene popped out of her own apartment across the breezeway.

Jilly tried for a lighthearted tone. "Just a couple of accidents up in the mountains."

"A *couple* of accidents?"

Right then, from inside, Jilly's house phone started ringing. She waved her paper at Orlene. "Phone. Gotta go. Take care." She backed up and shut her door on her staring neighbor, leaning against it briefly, promising herself that she would never so much as poke her head out that door again unless she had on a hat or a minimum of a week had passed. She figured by a week, the two goose eggs would have gone down and her bruises should yield, at least somewhat, to a heavy application of foundation.

Then again, maybe she was handling this all wrong. Maybe she should simply go boldly forth, let people gasp and exclaim over her all they wanted. They'd get over it. A lot sooner than she was going to.

Missy sat on the floor a few feet away, glaring up at her. The cat had yet to forgive her mistress for spiriting her away from Will.

And the phone was still ringing.

"Hello?"

"Happy New Year's Eve, Jilly."

"Ceil. How are you?"

"In labor."

At first, Jilly thought it must be a joke. "You're kidding, right?"

"No. My contractions are coming five minutes apart and Aaron and I are on the way to the hospital."

"Omigod. You mean you're in the car?"

"That's right."

"How are you? Are you—?"

"I'm fine. Poor Aaron, though. I don't know if he'll survive this."

Aaron said something at Celia's end of the line, but Jilly couldn't quite make it out.

Jilly smiled. "Tell him to take slow, deep breaths."

"I have. It didn't seem to help much—Janey's coming, with Cade. They're on their way."

Jilly clutched the phone a little tighter. She knew what her friend would say next.

"Oh, Jilly. Could you come, too?"

The problem was, she wanted to. She really, really wanted to. But Will might be there. And certainly Caitlin would. She didn't know if she was ready to deal with either of them just yet.

Celia coaxed, "I know you don't have much on your schedule till after the first, since you'd planned to stay up at Mavis's house until then. And it would be my treat. Just say yes and get to Sacramento International ASAP. We'll have a ticket waiting in your name for the next Las Vegas flight. And Aaron will send a car to pick you up at McCarran."

"Oh, that's crazy. You don't have to—"

"I want to. Every time I think of this baby, of how happy I am, I think of the three of us sitting by the fire at Janey's last February. I think of how I might never have had the nerve to go after what I wanted, if it hadn't been for you two."

"Ceil, I know you would have gone after that man on your own eventually."

Celia was laughing. "Sure, in another decade or two." Then she sighed. "It would mean so much to me—to have you here for this. Since the first day of kindergarten, whenever something major happened in my life, you and Janey were there. This is pretty major, you know? And I have to admit, I'd just like to see you. I've been a little worried about you since that mix-up last week over that old house of Mavis's."

Jilly winced. It was the problem with having really close friends—somehow they always sensed when something was wrong. "Oh, Ceil. Why? I really am okay. And the last thing you need right now is to be worrying about me."

"I can't help it. Janey says you never called her back about visiting her and Cade."

"She called me. We worked it out."

"I know. But you haven't called *me*."

"Ceil. Come on. It's only been a few days."

"Something's bothering you. I can sense—" Celia gasped. And the gasp became a low groan.

"Ceil. Are you okay?"

"Damn it, Jillian." Suddenly, it was Aaron growling in her ear. "She's having another contraction. Say you'll come so she can get off the phone and concentrate on having this baby."

When he put it like that, what else could she do? "All right. But I'll get my own flight." He started to growl some more. She said firmly, "I don't want you worrying about me. What hospital?" He told her. And she said, "Okay. Tell Celia I'll be there as soon as I possibly can."

"She's coming." He was talking to Celia now, his voice low, tender. And urgent. "Don't worry, my darling. She's on her way…."

Orlene promised to look after the sulking Missy. Jilly threw what she'd need for a couple of nights into a carry-on and found a cute, slouchy gray wool hat that covered most of the train wreck formerly known as her forehead. She locked up and went out and jumped in her 4Runner.

At the airport, the terminal smelled of Cinnabons. Jilly was practically salivating as she took her place in a very long ticket line, not holding out a lot of hope for getting a ticket at the last minute like this, on New Year's Eve. She was already resigning herself to calling Aaron back to report that she'd be driving in, after all.

But an hour later, when her turn came, she managed to get a flight with only a two-hour wait till takeoff. She couldn't believe her luck. And it wasn't even standby. She bought some magazines and an intriguing looking paperback mystery and then she surrendered to that delicious aroma and bought herself a huge, delectable cinnamon roll. She was just sitting down to devour it when the phone in her purse rang.

She checked the display before she answered. Great. "What do you want, Caitlin?"

"Hey, don't bother with a friendly tone. After all, it's only me."

"What do you want?"

"Aaron says you're on your way to Vegas."

"That's right."

"You got a flight?"

"I did."

"Way to go, sweetie pie. Listen, I want to be sure you get to the hospital in time to see my grandchild born. Give me your flight number. I'll have a car waiting to pick you up."

"Oh, Caitlin. I can see you coming a mile away."

"Now, darlin' girl, what is that supposed to mean?"

"You're up to something." Jilly didn't know exactly what, but it was Caitlin, so there had to be some kind of scheme going on here. Maybe she planned to trick poor Will into being the one to meet her at the airport. It seemed like a stretch, but with Caitlin, anything was possible.

"Jilly, sweetie, how come you're so damn suspicious lately?"

"Oh, puh-lease."

"Now, hon." Caitlin had put on a wheedling tone, one Jilly found particularly grating, given Caitlin's basic nature, which was brash and bossy in the extreme. "You just be a good girl and give me that flight number, now."

"Thanks, but I'll rent a car."

"That could be a problem," Caitlin advised in a sweet, husky singsong. "Darlin' girl, it's New Year's Eve."

"I'll manage. And I have to go. My Cinnabon is getting cold. Bye, now."

Caitlin was still wheedling away as she disconnected the call.

Jilly's flight took off on time and landed at McCarran right on schedule. She ran into a snag at the rental car booth. She'd called to reserve a car before her flight, but when she got there it turned out that available vehicles were nil. She thought of Caitlin, wondered if Will's manipulative mother could possibly have done something to keep her from getting her rental car.

But then how would Caitlin Bravo, who ran a saloon and café in a tiny town east of Tahoe, have that kind of influence with a Las Vegas rental car outlet? And why would she even want to do such a thing? Jilly must be getting paranoid. She'd have to watch that—though it was difficult to keep suspicions in check after you'd been dealing with Caitlin for a while.

Finally, about an hour after Jilly showed up at the desk, someone turned in a no-frills compact. Jilly snapped it up.

It took her forty-five minutes to reach the hospital from the airport. By then, it was three in the afternoon. She raced inside, stopped at the front desk for directions and then headed straight for the maternity ward.

When she stepped off the elevator, which opened right on to the waiting area, she knew she was in the right place. Celia's mom, Maggie Tuttle, sat in one of the gray chairs, wearing her usual sweetly distracted expression. Celia's oldest sister, Annie, sat beside Mrs. Tuttle, holding her mother's hand. Caitlin sat two chairs down from the Tuttle women. She was thumbing through a dog-eared magazine, her hard black hair gleaming, her black satin shirt spangled with sequins that perfectly matched her skin-tight turquoise jeans. Cade and Jane were there, too—Cade in baggy cargoes and a leather jacket, Jane in one of those Eddie Bauer jumpers that always looked just right on her, her coffee-colored hair a wild mass of cascading curls.

Oh, yes. Everyone who should be there *was* there. Except Aaron, who had taken labor classes with his wife and was probably with her right now. And Will…

Caitlin looked up first. "Darlin' Jilly. It's about time—and what's with the hat?"

"Hello, Caitlin." Jilly tipped her head back slightly

so she could see beneath the hat's low brim and gave Will's mother a big, defiant smile.

"Hey, there," said Cade.

Celia's mother let out a tired littler chirp of greeting, and Annie gave Jilly a nod and a smile.

Janey jumped from her chair, arms outstretched. Jilly rushed to her. They met in a hug. "I was getting worried," Janey whispered once they had their arms around each other.

Jilly gave her other best friend one more good squeeze and stepped back. "Nothing to worry about. Here I am, safe and sound."

"Is this some hot, new look?" Janey brushed the low brim of the hat. "How do you see?"

"I tip my head back. Tell me. How's Ceil? Has the baby arrived?"

"Not yet."

"Is everything going okay?"

"So far as we know. Evidently, things have slowed down. But there's nothing to worry about. The baby's fine and Ceil is, too."

Maggie Tuttle sighed. "First babies. They always take forever." Celia's mother ought to know. She'd had six babies herself.

Caitlin stood. "Jilly honey, it'll be a while before we get anymore news. And I'll bet you're dyin' for a snack about now. I've checked out the cafeteria and they've got bacon burgers and fairly decent fries. It ain't the Highgrade, but it'll do in a pinch. How about if you and me head on down to the cafeteria?"

Jilly grabbed Jane's hand. There was no way she was

letting Caitlin Bravo corner her alone. "Thanks so much. But Janey'll take me. We have some catching up to do, anyway."

Jane was a champion. She didn't miss a beat. "Do we ever. This way."

"Don't you leave me alone with her," Jilly said desperately.

Jane had led her to a quiet corner, where they could talk undisturbed. Jilly had her bacon burger and fries in front of her and her head tipped way back so she could see her friend across the table.

"I'll do what I can." Jane tore the top off a container of strawberry-kiwi yogurt. "And I am sorry. But she really thinks you're the one for Will, and when Caitlin decides you're right for one of her boys..." Jane's voice trailed off and she shook that cloud of thick, dark hair. "She'll get over it. In time. And Jilly, come on. What is going on with that hat?"

It was one hat comment too many. Jilly gave in and took the hat off.

Jane said, "My God."

"I think of it this way, in six or eight weeks, who's gonna know I ever looked this bad?"

"How did it happen?"

"Got a month?"

Jane leaned closer, dark eyes shining with love and concern. Jilly felt a little better, just to have so much caring coming her way. "I want to hear," Jane said. "Everything. Please. It's what friends are for, you know?"

"We should get back soon. Ceil might—"

"If they need us or she wants us, they know where to find us."

"It seems...I don't know, like a bad idea, to tell you about it."

Janey had no trouble understanding why. "Because it's about Will, right? And his brother is my husband."

Jilly felt her face turning red. "Yeah, 'fraid so."

And Janey said, "I'm your friend. It feels to me that we've *always* been friends. You know in the end you'll have to come to me or to Ceil—and Ceil is married to one of Will's brother's, too. So what can you do?"

Jilly picked up a French fry and set it down without eating it. "Oh, Janey. I just don't know...."

A sudden frown drew Janey's brows together. "You're not trying to tell me...Will didn't...?"

"What?" Jilly pointed to her forehead. *"This?"*

Janey now wore a look of pure horror. She gulped. Nodded.

Jilly cried "No! Of course Will didn't do this to me." It hurt, she realized, just to say his name out loud. Tears tightened her throat. "He only *thinks* that he did."

Jane set down her yogurt and laid her hand over Jilly's. "Come on, now. You'd better explain."

So Jilly did. She told it all. How she and Will despised each other at first, how the tree branch fell on her, how she told Will she'd overheard him saying rude things about her, how Mavis appeared in her dreams. She included the part about how Missy went missing, and the night Will told her about Nora and then the lights went out. She explained how Mavis showed her where to find Missy. And then she shared a little about the best times—the Christmas she and Will had made, just the two of them, his birthday the next day....

Jane leaned close across the table. "You became lovers, then?"

"Yes." And Jilly told the rest, about the lost dog they never found and how she fell into a ravine chasing after him. How everything changed after that. How Will sent her away—but then had to go and give her that one last incredible kiss, out in the clearing, as she was leaving. How he insisted she call him to say she'd made it home safe.

When she was done, Janey said, "So what now?"

"I don't have any idea."

Janey was smiling. "I think you do. I think maybe Caitlin's right about you and Will. I think maybe you think so, too."

"Oh, God. You think?"

"How could I not? Look at all that's happened. Even Mad Mavis is trying to get you two together."

"Don't even joke about that. I mean, that is seriously creepy. I sincerely did feel that she really *was* there, that she was trying to help Will, you know, from beyond the grave?"

Jane shrugged. "Maybe she was. And if she was, well, isn't that kind of wonderful?"

"Oh, Janey. You think?"

Jane leaned close again. "Maybe you just have to... accept it. Just take whatever lesson you believe you were supposed to learn from it and go with it." She picked up her yogurt and sat back in her chair. "Eat your burger."

"I will." Jilly reached for it. But before she took a bite,

she set it down again. "Where *is* he? Do you know? Is he still up at Mavis's house? Did anyone call him? Does he realize that his first niece or nephew is, at this very moment, being born?"

Jane spooned up more yogurt. "I assume he's still at the cabin. And yes, he's been told about the baby. Aaron finally got hold of him. I think Caitlin called him about a hundred times. She left message after message. She finally badgered Aaron into calling and that call, Will answered."

"But he's not coming?"

Jane gave her a patient look. "Jilly, think about it. A baby's birth is not really the kind of thing bachelor uncles feel obligated to attend—especially not when they have to get to the hospital from high in the mountains five hundred miles away."

"Not coming..."

Jane gave her a sympathetic look. "No, I don't think so."

Oh, why did she feel so deflated and sad? She'd been telling herself that what she wanted most was *not* to have to see him.

Jane was leaning forward again. "Jilly..."

"Is this advice I'm about to get?"

"Yes, it is. Are you listening?"

"Oh, yes. Yes, I am."

"When it comes to love, *somebody's* got to go for it, to stand up and say, 'This is what I want and I intend to fight for it.' Caitlin told me that."

"You're kidding."

"No. My mother-in-law does have her honestly in-sightful moments."

"You're saying I should fight for Will?"

"I'm saying you two won't work anything out if you never see each other. I'm saying if you have something to say to him, you ought to track him down and say it. You can't allow yourself to imagine that the opportunity to work things out with him is somehow going to drop into your lap."

David Aaron Bravo, ten pounds, three ounces and twenty-one inches long, was born at ten minutes past midnight on the first day of the New Year. After mother and child were cleaned up and settled in their own private room, the anxious visitors who'd waited all those hours for the baby's arrival were allowed in to see them, one or two at a time, for only a few minutes each. The new mother asked to see Jane and Jillian together.

Jilly's first thought when she entered that hospital room was that Celia looked awful. She had dark circles beneath her eyes. Her red hair, hanging lank and oily on her shoulders, cried out for a shampoo and some decent conditioning. The hideous floral hospital gown had to go.

Ungroomed, exhausted and unattractively dressed, Ceil also somehow managed to look luminous. She gazed down at her child with so much love and pride on her heart-shaped face, that Jilly found herself gulping furiously to keep from bursting into tears.

Celia glanced up and a sharp cry of distress escaped her. "Jilly. What's happened?"

Jilly touched her forehead. "Oh, this? It's nothing. A tree branch fell on me and I rolled down a ravine."

"But you're okay?"

Jilly shared a look with Jane, then announced, "Never better."

"And we'll only stay a second," Jane vowed.

Ceil was smiling again. "It's so good to see you both." And then she whispered, "Triple threat."

Jane and Jilly repeated the words in unison. "Triple threat."

It was what they used to call themselves, way back when, as kids. In reality, of course, they'd been no threat to anyone. They were three nice girls who, for the most part, had spent their lives behaving themselves.

Jane and Jilly moved in to get a closer look at David Aaron.

"Oh, I cannot believe those tiny hands," Jilly whispered. "That incredible perfect little mouth...." She offered her index finger and one of those waving hands wrapped reflexively around it.

Ceil said, "Janey, did you talk to her?"

Jilly caressed the baby's gripping fingers with a brushing motion of her thumb. "She did. I told her everything. And as usual, *she'll* tell *you* everything I said."

Jane chuckled. "But later. After you've rested."

Ceil said, "Jilly, you *could* just tell me yourself."

And Jane said, "She can't. In a few minutes, she's leaving."

Reluctantly, Jilly pulled her finger free of David Aaron's grip.

"Leaving?" Celia adjusted the blanket around

her new baby's darling wrinkled face. "Where is she going?" And then she looked up and grinned. "Never mind. I think I can guess."

Caitlin caught up with her as she was heading for the elevators. "Jilly. Hold up. Don't even imagine you're getting away from here without—"

Jilly turned and grabbed Will's mother and hugged her for all she was worth. "Gotta go. See you soon."

For once in her life, Caitlin Bravo actually seemed a loss for words.

The elevator door was already open. Jilly stepped through. The door closed just as she turned and gave Caitlin a wave.

Outside it was sixty degrees. A beautiful winter's night in Las Vegas. Jilly sucked in a big breath of the balmy, smoggy air and headed for her car.

But there was a problem. The space where she'd left her no-frills compact rental had a huge midnight-blue Chevy Suburban in it now.

Was it possible that someone would actually go to the trouble of stealing a car like the one she had rented?

Maybe this was just a mistake. She'd been careful to write down the level and row number on a piece of paper, since more than once in her life, she'd lost track of where she'd parked her car in the first place.

But not this time. Right level, right row.

Wrong vehicle.

She heard a car approaching, rolling slowly her way. She turned and put up a hand against the glare of the headlights. The car kept coming, slowing to a stop right beside her.

She saw that it was a Mercedes. G-Class. Very dirty, a car that had recently covered a lot of distance on muddy roads. But underneath the mud, it was silver.

Will rolled the driver's-side window down. "Need a lift?"

Chapter 17

Her heart was doing impossible things inside her chest. And the world was suddenly so vivid. So beautiful. The parking garage seemed to shimmer with loveliness.

Yet she spoke quite calmly. "What are you doing here?"

"Aaron said you would be here. I came to find you."

She stared at him, narrow-eyed. Then she blinked. "You're serious."

"As a blow to the head. As a long roll down a steep ravine."

"That's pretty serious." She looked at him sideways. "Would your mother go so far as grand theft auto, do you think?"

"Hmm," he said. "We *are* talking about Caitlin, which means anything's possible."

She saw movement behind him. She blinked again.

But the brown-and-white spotted dog on the seat beside him was still there, ears perked, panting contentedly. "Oh, Will. You found him...."

There was a moment. A shimmering, private, perfect moment. Will looked at her and she looked back. It was magic.

It was love.

Finally, Will said, "The truth is, *he* found *me*. I opened the door. There he was. I started calling him Snapper, for no reason in particular. He didn't object, so that's his name."

She had never been quite this happy in her life. "You mean—you're keeping him? You've got a dog, at last?"

"I would have to say it's more that *he's* keeping me. He's why I *drove* down. Hard enough to get a flight at New Year's without a dog to worry about."

She thought of David Aaron. "Did you hear—about the baby?"

He shook his head. "I've been leaving my phone turned off a lot. Caitlin's always calling. I get sick of hearing it ring."

She told him the news.

"Well," he said, a musing half smile on that wonderful face. "What do you know? I'm an uncle."

They looked at each other again, just stared and grinned until a car drove up behind him and honked to let them know they were blocking the flow of traffic.

Will said, "Let's go."

She rushed around to the passenger's side. Snapper jumped in back without even having to be told. "Where are we going?" Not that she really cared.

"Some place where we can talk."

* * *

In Las Vegas, finding a decent hotel in the middle of the night presented no problem. They paid a hefty extra fee in order to be allowed to have Snapper in the suite with them.

Once the three of them were alone, Jilly fussed over the dog for a few minutes, then Will ordered him to go lie down. Snapper trotted right over to the sofa against the far wall and made himself comfortable.

Will took her by the shoulders. "You won't believe this. I keep having these dreams. Of my dead grandmother. Of Nora. Last night, I finally put it all together. My grandmother wants me to be with you."

"I *do* believe it. I had a few nighttime encounters with Mavis myself."

"You're not serious."

"Oh, but I am. And I have to admit, the whole experience had me seriously spooked. But yesterday I talked to Janey about it. She said what I needed to do was to accept it, to learn whatever lesson I thought Mavis might be trying to teach me."

"I always did like Jane. She's woman with both feet firmly on the ground."

"Not silly and flighty like some of us."

"Silly and flighty? No damn way. Lighthearted. Eager. So very, very *alive*." He had her face cradled in his hands. He kissed her. A kiss that burned her to a joyful cinder and melted her into a puddle of love and desire. Simultaneously.

But there was still more to talk about before they could make use of the big bed a few feet away.

She broke the kiss. "And Nora?"

He gave her a crooked, musing grin. "It took me a while to get what she was trying to say to me."

"Because?"

"I kept dreaming of her off in the distance, waving, telling me something I couldn't make out. And then, last night, I got it. I understood she was saying goodbye. She was saying—"

Jilly knew. "That her dying was not your fault."

He grabbed her close again, his strong arms banding tight around her. "I did know it." He whispered the words into her hair. "In my mind. It's just...taken a while for the knowledge to settle into my heart."

Jilly hugged him as hard as her arms could hug.

And then he was taking her shoulders again, holding her away enough that he could see her face. "Luckily, this Christmas, I got professional help."

She laughed at that. "It was a hell of a job, but somebody had to do it. And for my fee..."

"Anything."

She laid a finger against those warm, tempting lips. "Don't say that until you've heard what I want."

He grabbed her hand, kissed that finger. "Anything," he repeated. "Name your price."

So she did. "I love you, Will. Marry me."

He said, "You're crazy."

"No. It's time for the big leap of faith. For both of us. I'm scared to death and I know you are, too. But I think that you do love me. And as I've just told you, I love you. So..."

He grabbed her close again, even tighter than before. "But what if—"

"No. None of it, none of the bad things that have happened in the past were your fault."

"But you have to admit—"

"I admit nothing, not when it comes to this. I messed up once, badly, when I chose a man to love. But I'm not letting that wrong choice keep me from making the *right* choice now. And *you* can't let the bad things that have happened to you keep you from reaching out and grabbing hold when a good thing comes your way. Oh, Will, there's just no way for us to know how it's all going to turn out, what will happen next year, tomorrow, an hour from now. All we can do is live for all we're worth, from minute to minute."

"You seem so damn sure."

"I *am* sure. About this, anyway. You are no jinx, Will Bravo. You are the man that I love."

"I really like the sound of that."

"I'm glad. Because it would take a lot more than your bad luck to do me in. I lived through this holiday season at your side. And I intend to live through a lifetime more of them."

"Is that a promise?"

"It is a vow."

"I love you, Jilly. Marry me."

She sighed. "Missy is going to be so very pleased."

"Kiss me, damn it."

Jilly did. With tenderness and heat, sweetness and sizzle. And with all the love in her heart.

* * *

They ended up in the bed for several long, lovely hours.

But luckily, it was Las Vegas. They got up at noon and called Jilly's mother to give her the news. Next, they called Aaron, who put Celia on to congratulate them. Then they tracked down Jane and Cade to be their witnesses. Caitlin got wind of a wedding in the works. She insisted on being there, too. She also swore she'd had nothing to do with the disappearance of Jilly's rental car, which turned up a few days later—in Winnemucca, of all places.

Thus, in a very short time, everything was arranged. And at six in the evening, on the first day of January, Jilly Diamond and Will Bravo exchanged their wedding vows at the Chapel of Love Eternal in the heart of Las Vegas, right on the Strip.

Epilogue

On December twenty-second of that year, Jillian and Will Bravo put their cat and their dog and a whole lot of groceries into Will's Mercedes and drove up into the mountains.

The old house seemed to be waiting just for them. They cut down their own tree and decorated it with all the wonderful faded ornaments in Mavis's attic. Will read the first two hundred pages of *The Brothers Karamazov*. Jilly got in a little work on some future columns. She beat him at Scrabble and he trounced her at checkers. They listened to NPR and Christmas carols. For the most part, Missy and Snapper got along.

There was Dinty Moore chili and Campbell's tomato soup, Kraft macaroni and cheese and bags and bags of Cheez Doodles. For Christmas, they prepared the kind of meal that would have made the divine Martha proud.

And they made love. Frequently. With great joy.

If Will seemed reluctant to let Jilly out of his sight, she tried to be tolerant of his not-quite-banished fears. Life, after all, was a work in progress. And old ways of thinking sometimes died hard.

As midnight approached on December thirty-first, they filled their juice glasses with the finest champagne. When the clock on the old desk in the corner said the New Year had come, they raised their glasses high.

Will proposed the toast. "To us, to our first anniversary. And to one entire holiday season injury-free."

"I'll drink to that."

They drained their glasses.

She put her hand over his. "It's going to get easier as every year goes by."

"Is that a promise?"

"It is a vow. Now, kiss me, damn it."

And he did.

* * * * *

FAMOUS FAMILIES

YES! Please send me the *Famous Families* collection featuring the Fortunes, the Bravos, the McCabes and the Cavanaughs. This collection will begin with 3 FREE BOOKS and 2 FREE GIFTS in my very first shipment—and more valuable free gifts will follow! My books will arrive in 8 monthly shipments until I have the entire 51-book *Famous Families* collection. I will receive 2-3 free books in each shipment and I will pay just $4.49 U.S./$5.39 CDN for each of the other 4 books in each shipment, plus $2.99 for shipping and handling.* If I decide to keep the entire collection, I'll only have paid for 32 books because 19 books are free. I understand that accepting the 3 free books and gifts places me under no obligation to buy anything. I can always return a shipment and cancel at any time. My free books and gifts are mine to keep no matter what I decide.

268 HCN 9971   468 HCN 9971

Name _____ (PLEASE PRINT)

Address _____ Apt. #

City _____ State/Prov. _____ Zip/Postal Code

Signature (if under 18, a parent or guardian must sign)

Mail to the **Reader Service**:
IN U.S.A.: P.O. Box 1867, Buffalo, NY 14240-1867
IN CANADA: P.O. Box 609, Fort Erie, Ontario L2A 5X3

* Terms and prices subject to change without notice. Prices do not include applicable taxes. Sales tax applicable in N.Y. Canadian residents will be charged applicable taxes. This offer is limited to one order per household. All orders subject to approval. Credit or debit balances in a customer's account(s) may be offset by any other outstanding balance owed by or to the customer. Please allow 4 to 6 weeks for delivery. Offer available while quantities last. Offer not available to Quebec residents.

Your Privacy- The Reader Service is committed to protecting your privacy. Our Privacy Policy is available online at www.ReaderService.com or upon request from the Reader Service.
We make a portion of our mailing list available to reputable third parties that offer products we believe may interest you. If you prefer that we not exchange your name with third parties, or if you wish to clarify or modify your communication preferences, please visit us at www.ReaderService.com/consumerschoice or write to us at Reader Service Preference Service, P.O. Box 9062, Buffalo, NY 14269. Include your complete name and address.

FFBPA11